N

Also available in Large Print
by Ray Hogan:

Iron Jehu
Raptors
Doomsday Trail
Ragans Law
*The Doomsday Marshal and the Hanging
   Judge*
Outlaw's Empire
The Rawhiders
The Doomsday Canyon
The Doomsday Bullet
Lawman's Choice

Ray Hogan

THE CROSSHATCH MEN

G.K.HALL &CO.
Boston, Massachusetts
1992

For my wife—
LOIS

Copyright © 1989 by Ray Hogan.

Published in Large Print by arrangement with
Doubleday, a division of
Bantam Doubleday Dell Publishing Group, Inc.

G.K. Hall Large Print Book Series.

Set in 16 pt. Plantin.

Library of Congress Cataloging-in-Publication Data

Hogan, Ray, 1908–
    The crosshatch men / Ray Hogan.
      p. cm.—(G.K. Hall large print books)
    ISBN 0-8161-5275-6 (lg. print)
    1. Large type books. I. Title.
PS3558.O3473C75 1992
813′.54—dc20

                                   91-28252

The wind blowing down across the low hills and flats from the Mimbres Mountains to the north still had a touch of winter in it. There was snow on nearby Cooke's Peak to the west and small patches of white could be seen on the lower crest of its companion, Massacre Mountain—all of which was unusual for so late in the spring.

Curt Ramsey slumped in the leather chair that his uncle, Jubilee Jackson, had built for him, stared moodily through the dusty window of the ranch house kitchen. Cursing in a low, angry voice and without shifting his eyes, he changed the position of his outstretched legs, useless for over two years now, after his horse had reared suddenly at the unexpected appearance of a cougar and thrown him hard onto a ragged pile of broken rocks.

Abruptly his cursing ceased. His head came up. "Something's wrong," he muttered. "Hell, ain't nothing gone right around here since I got myself busted up!"

Jackson, moving the small pot of coffee that Calderone, the aging cook, had brought

in earlier to the back of the stove where it would keep warm, turned. A tall, bent, hawk-faced man with near-colorless blue eyes and a stringy mustache, he had been Curt's sole source of physical support, confidant, and whipping boy since the accident.

"What do you mean—something's wrong?"

"Just what I said, goddamnit!" Ramsey snapped. "The crew's coming in and it's too early for that. And they've got somebody hanging across a saddle. Wheel me out onto the porch."

Silent, Jubilee crossed the room to the wheelbarrow he had converted into a makeshift but serviceable wheelchair and, taking up the handles, pushed it over beside Curt. Putting his arms around the wasted figure of the rancher, he lifted him clear of the chair and sat him in the padded boxlike affair. Several times he had suggested to Curt that he buy himself a regular wheelchair, available in El Paso some fifty miles to the south, but Ramsey would not hear of it. His legs would eventually mend, grow strong, and become dependable again, he was certain—an assumption that would never come to pass, according to the doctor.

"Come on! Come on!" Ramsey ranted,

impatience coloring his square face. "Want to get out there before they ride in."

Jackson, opening the door that led out onto the porch that ran across the rear width of the Crosshatch ranch house, shook his head.

"Don't get all het up. Ain't no cause to rush—they ain't even close—and besides, they're coming here, ain't they?"

"Not saying they ain't, but it's only fitting that I be out there when they come in."

"You will be, but if you ain't they'll wait," Jackson said mildly and, taking up the handles of the improvised wheelchair, pushed the rancher out into the brisk afternoon breeze.

"Put me over there at the edge of the porch," Curt directed. "Can you see who all it is?"

Two of the dogs that hung around the ranch trotted up, tails wagging, ears lifted expectantly. Over in the cookshack Calderone was preparing the evening meal for the dozen or so hands that Crosshatch employed and over to the south of the yard a meadowlark perched on a fence post was whistling defiantly into the cool breeze.

"Ain't but about half the crew," Jubilee said, squinting into the afternoon glare.

"I can count, damnit!" Curt snapped. "What I'm wanting to know is who are they—and what's wrong."

"Can see Phin Durbin. And there's Joe Abbot and Bill Toon. Can't tell who the two other birds are."

"What about the one slung across his saddle?"

"Can't figure that out, his head hanging down like it is."

"There's been trouble again with them Mexican bandits," Curt said and swore deeply. "Or maybe them Comanches are back again. I wish to hell we had some law around here that'd look after a man's property."

"Expect what we got tries. Trouble is we're so close to the border. Them bandits and Comanches can just run back and forth easy as pie."

"Ought to get more lawmen down here then," Curt grumbled.

Only a few years past thirty, Curt Ramsey showed the ravages of his disability in both body and face. With lifeless brown hair, dull eyes, hollow features further blighted by a neglected graying beard and mustache, he was down to a low one hundred thirty pounds from a normal one hundred and eighty. Dressed as usual in denim pants, coarse, woolen shirt of faded blue, and flat-heeled boots that he pulled on every morning despite his inability to walk, he was a man stubbornly refusing to accept the inevitable. He had spent his entire life, once out of childhood years, at the grueling labor of raising cattle and could not now adapt himself without rancor and bitterness to one as a helpless observer.

"If that damn Boone and Jesse hadn't run off like they did," he muttered, "this here ranch wouldn't be in the shape it's in."

Jubilee turned to the rancher in surprise. It was the first time he'd heard Curt mention his two brothers, once partners with him in Crosshatch, in years. Both had pulled up stakes a decade ago, unable and unwilling to take Curt's continual abuse as well as that of Ramsey's wife, Elvira, who had since died.

"Yeah, I reckon things would," Jackson said. He added wryly, "You happen to know where they are?"

"You know goddamn well I don't!" Curt shouted. "And I sure wouldn't ask them for help if I did. Was their own doings to pull out on me. Now they can damn well stay out."

The oncoming riders had rounded the corner of the holding corral and were entering the yard. Phin Durbin was now out front leading the horse that was carrying the draped body of the dead man. The remaining Crosshatch riders ranged behind them in a loose half circle.

Curt watched narrowly as the men drew near and then halted at the end of the porch. Durbin came down off the bay gelding he was riding and nodded to Curt.

"Got some real bad news for you, Mr. Ramsey," he said.

"Who is it?" Curt demanded impatiently, trying to make out the identity of the man hanging across the calico horse.

"George Coe—"

"Coe!" Ramsey shouted in a shocked voice.

"Yeah, found him down on the south range where them rocky hills are. He'd been shot in the back."

"Them goddamn Mex bandits—some of their work!" Curt said. "Any cattle missing?"

Durbin, a square-built, husky red-haired man just into his thirties, shrugged. He was a hard case, strong, considered expert with the gun he carried, and was something of a bully. He had a broad, ruddy face and a sandy mustache, and dressed in the usual garb of a working cowhand—cord pants, checkered flannel shirt, neckerchief, vest, stovepipe boots, and a high crowned hat.

"Can't tell for certain, Mr. Ramsey, but I've been missing some right along. Little jag here, little jag there. My guess is that whoever it was got away with a few steers—maybe even more'n I think."

Jubilee turned to Curt. He didn't like Phin Durbin, had never trusted the man from the day he'd come to work on Cross-hatch some two years ago. At that moment Calderone, stained once-white apron pulled up about his hips, came out of the cook-shack with his arms folded across his narrow chest and leaned back against the wall to watch.

"George never said nothing about any steers missing," Jackson commented.

"Hate to say this, Mr. Ramsey, but George Coe ain't been doing much of a job for you lately. Anyway, you're running about three thousand head, more or less. Kind of hard to miss a couple of dozen."

"Coe always done a good job for me," Curt said, shaking his head at Durbin. "Been my foreman for a lot of years. Never had no cause to fault him—not for anything."

"Sure, sure, whatever you say," Durbin remarked with a shrug. Turning his head, he glanced over his shoulder at the men behind him. "I ain't one to do no talking about a dead man . . . What do you want me to do with his body? Take it into town for burying?"

"No," Curt answered, "I don't want him put in that boneyard in Mesilla. Take him over to where the family's buried."

"Where he belongs," Jubilee agreed.

The men, one leading the dead man's horse, wheeled about and struck off in the direction of the bunkhouse and the family cemetery lying on a slight hill beyond.

"Mr. Ramsey, maybe this ain't exactly the right time to speak up, but I can take over Coe's job as—"

"No!" Jubilee Jackson cut in sharply, a frown twisting his features. "I—"

Ramsey swung about to face Jackson. "Since when do you do any deciding around here?" he demanded angrily. "You're forgetting you're just one of the hired hands."

"I ain't forgetting that. It's just that—"

Durbin smiled faintly. He nodded. "Know you were figuring on Coe driving a thousand head to Wichita for selling this spring. Can do that for you. I know the trail. Been on quite a few drives."

Jubilee looked at Ramsey and shook his head. "Best you let me handle that, Curt."

The rancher's jaw hardened. "This here ranch is still mine, crippled up or not," he said. "Means I'm still able to run it. If you—"

"I'm just figuring you ought to hold off a spell, do some thinking about it before you go making Durbin—or anyone else —foreman."

The squat redhead cast an angry glance at Jackson. "I reckon Mr. Ramsey knows what he's doing," he said. Then he added in a low breath, "Stay out of this, old man."

Ramsey did not hear. He was looking off across the hardpack to the plain beyond, fresh and green from the spring rains.

"I sure do," the rancher said after a few moments. "You've got the job, Phin. We'll do some talking about it later."

Jubilee brushed wearily at the stubble on his chin. "You're making a mistake, Curt," he said and turned away.

2

Curt Ramsey watched in silence as Jubilee and the cook, Caspar Calderone, began to fill in George Coe's grave. Durbin and the rest of the crew had gone, some returning to the range, others to the bunkhouse where they would take their ease until time for supper, after which they would ride out for nighthawk duty.

"We will eat late tonight, *patrón*," Calderone said, wiping at the sweat on his dark face as he paused to lean on the shovel he was using. "This burying will take much time."

"Then go on back to your kitchen!" Ramsey snapped irritably. "Jubilee can take care of this."

Calderone, short, squat, large teeth showing whitely between his thick lips, bobbed. Tossing the shovel aside, he threw an apologetic glance at Jackson, turned, and hurried off across the hardpack.

"When you get through with that shoveling I want you to pull them weeds growing there on Pa's grave—Ma's too," Curt said. "I'd do it myself was I able."

Pa and Ma would like it if they knew he was seeing to the care of their graves, Ramsey thought. They set great store in such things—a peculiarity that he had always found hard to understand. Dead was dead, and anybody being dead sure as hell didn't know what was going on in the world they had left!

His pa, Eben—Ebenezer—and his ma, Tildy, had come west back in the early sixties, taking advantage of Abraham Lincoln's Homestead Act. Tildy's brother Jubilee had come with them, and together they had filed claim on adjoining parcels of land.

Almost immediately trouble had risen. The Spanish and Mexican people had claimed prior ownership based on grants from the King of Spain. Determined to hang onto their land, Eben, leaving their budding ranch in the care of Tildy and their young sons and accompanied by Jubilee, made the long trip to Santa Fe, the territory's capital, where they hoped to clear up the disputes.

Such grants from Spain had all been verified and settled by General Stephen Kearny back in the late 1840s, they were told; and the land they had settled on, as well as thousands of other acres in that particular vicinity, either was not included in the grants or had been forfeited by the grantee, who had failed to register ownership in the period of time specified by those in charge of reorganizing the territory. Thus assured, Eben and Jubilee returned to their holdings and began development and expansion in earnest.

Eventually Jackson had grown weary of working his property. Despite the fact he had several good cowhands, he discovered he had no talent for being a boss and running a ranch successfully. Finally giving up, he sold out to Eben and Tildy and moved in with them and their three sons. There, lacking the iron-jawed, hard-fisted traits that constitute a good foreman, he became a sort of handyman, overseer, and errand boy.

But Jubilee was happy with the job and Eben, immersed in the constant task of building up his ranch, was grateful for his help. For one thing, Jackson kept an eye on the boys, actually becoming a second father to them, according to a remark Tildy had once made.

She had died in 1870, Eben in 1875, Curt recalled, his attention still on Jubilee. The older man had finished mounding the grave, placed the wooden marker with George Coe and the date burned into it at its upper end, and was now busy pulling the weeds that had all but taken over the final resting places of Eben and Tildy.

Eben had left Crosshatch, as he had named his ranch, to his three sons, designating Curt as head of the one-hundred-thousand-acre spread. The ranch had grown strong and prosperous under the guidance and industry of the elder Ramsey, and Curt, a duplication of his father in all ways, had taken charge immediately, with the result that the ranch had continued along its successful path.

Maybe he should have never married, Curt mused, for things changed between him and his two brothers soon after. He had never really been close to either of them, nor had they been to each other, but they had worked as a family, pulling as one for the good of Crosshatch, always conscious of the blood ties that linked them together.

Curt had particularly disliked Boone, who was next to him in age and who had often challenged his judgment, and he cared even less for Jesse who, while usually doing his share of work on the ranch, spent as much time as possible gambling with the hired help and further honing his expertise with cards by sitting in with the professionals in Mesilla and Las Cruces.

Boone was always the quiet, stubborn sort who did things his way or not at all. He had a way with the six-gun he'd provided himself with and spent much time—and money—practicing a fast draw and accuracy. Curt recalled how time after time, while he was busy at some chore, he would hear distant gunshots which meant that Boone was off in some arroyo developing his skill with the .45.

But his problems with Boone and Jesse came to an end two, or perhaps it was three years ago, after he had married Elvira Cartwright. Daughter of a Mesilla merchant, she quickly took a major hand in running Crosshatch, making good use of her sarcastic wit and sharp tongue.

At first it had amused Curt to hear her cut Boone or Jesse down to size, berate them for not being of more use on the ranch, or chastise them generally for leaving the burden of running the ranch wholly on her husband's shoulders. But eventually he, too, grew weary of the woman's constant carping and, when Boone had suddenly gotten his fill and ridden off, to be followed a year later by Jesse, he was not surprised.

In fact, he was relieved. Now there would be some peace in the house, he had assured himself, and there was. Elvira, a slender woman with piercing dark eyes, seemed satisfied that his two brothers were no longer around, so much so that he had wondered several times if his wife had not set out intentionally to drive them off. Whatever, things were better and all ran smoothly, as Elvira never dared to try her insulting ways on him.

Crosshatch continued to grow. He had accumulated more land, increased the water supply by widening the stream that flowed off the Berrendo, and further improved matters by buying a couple of Fresno scrapers and cutting a ditch northeast to connect the Rio Grande with a natural hollow lying in the heart of several small hills, thus providing ample water for cattle grazing in the section of Crosshatch range.

Elvira died in 1882, her departure leaving him lonely and somewhat embittered. To mitigate his loss he began to concentrate even more intensely on the ranch, increasing the size of the herd, which now numbered over three thousand head, building more corrals and other needed sheds, enlarging the house and barn, and acquiring additional range.

And then that goddamned horse had fallen on him.

His resulting condition—a life without use of his legs—was what made George Coe so valuable to him, along with Jubilee, of course. He would have liked it if Jubilee could have become his foreman, but he was not strong enough to take charge of running Crosshatch; it took a hard nose like Coe, or a hard case like Phin Durbin. Naturally if Boone and Jesse had still been around like they should have been, he'd have no big problem. Boone could handle the men, and likely Jesse could too, if he'd settle down and put his mind to it.

"Curt, I was wanting to talk to you about the foreman's job," Ramsey heard Jubilee say. "Didn't have no chance there a bit ago to tell you what I was thinking."

Ramsey shifted on the padded seat of the wheelbarrow. Jubilee had made the arrangement as comfortable as possible by building a slanted back inside the vehicle's box, knocking out the front, and extending the bed so that his legs could be stretched out before him.

"What about the foreman's job? Already told Durbin—"

"Know that—and I sure don't cotton to the idea. I plain don't trust him."

"You got a reason to say that?"

"Yep, reckon I have. Coe told me once that every now and then a few steers would turn up missing, eight or maybe ten head."

"So? Rustling around here ain't new," Ramsey said irritably. "Between the Mexicans coming across the border and the Indians riding down from—"

"They ain't who Coe figured was doing it."

"Who the hell then? Come on, what're you trying to say?"

"He figured it was Durbin and that bunch that runs with him."

Curt Ramsey frowned, rubbed at the two days' growth of whiskers on his chin. The afternoon had faded and the shadows of the cottonwoods planted around the little cemetery were beginning to lengthen.

"Now, George never said nothing like that to me. You for damn sure about it?"

"I asked him if he'd told you, he said no, he didn't have no proof, but he was working on it. Said that soon as he had something to go on, he was aiming to talk to you. Whole thing's got me to puzzling it over. Just maybe George did find out something on Durbin—and finding it out got him a bullet in the back."

Curt's features hardened. "You saying you think Durbin shot George in the back?"

"Just saying that could be what happened. I know you don't figure I'm man enough to take over for you—but you could give it to Dan Payne. He's been around long enough to—"

"Same reason I can't turn it over to you. He's too old. Crew wouldn't pay no mind to him. Anyway I—"

"Mr. Ramsey, you want me to go right ahead being your foreman starting now? If you're still figuring to drive a herd to Wichita, I ought to start making plans right now."

Curt swung his attention about at the sound of Phin Durbin's voice. Just how long the man had been standing there, apparently having walked over from the bunkhouse, he could only guess, but there was nothing to be done about it now. Anyway, he didn't give a good goddamn. Letting Durbin know in a roundabout way that he'd be keeping an eye on him was a good idea.

Ramsey glanced at Jubilee. Jackson had

a scowl on his craggy features, making it plain he was solidly against Phin Durbin and would continue to be so. The hell with Jubilee! Crosshatch was his and he'd run it to suit himself.

"Yeah, take over, Phin," he said, leaning back in the wheelbarrow. "I'm leaving it up to you to keep the men working and the place going right . . . And figure on that drive—a thousand head. Might as well start cutting them out."

The squat foreman nodded. "Sure thing, Mr. Ramsey. I'll get right on it—and you can depend on me doing things just the way you want."

"Fine. I'll be holding you to that," Curt said, and shifted his attention to Jubilee. "Get me over to the house—and get me some supper. I'm hungry."

3

Jubilee Jackson took up the handles of the wheelbarrow and started down the slight slope for the ranch house, lying on the far side of the hardpack. It was useless to talk to Curt about not signing on Phin Durbin as foreman, he could see that, but he was thoroughly convinced that turning the job over to the husky redhead was a mistake that could only lead to trouble and possibly disaster for Crosshatch.

"Sure wish you'd back off from—" he began as they drew near the edge of the yard, but Ramsey cut him short.

"If you're going to say I was wrong making Phin my foreman, save your breath! He's the man I want and I ain't changing my mind."

"Damnit, Curt, he'll steal you blind!" Jubilee said impatiently, coming flat out with his convictions. "Already been doing that working the range. Now that you've gone and made him boss of the whole kit and kaboodle, he'll fatten himself up real fast!"

"That's only what you think," Curt said indifferently. "You ain't got the proof, and that's what counts with me. Could be you're doing all this bellyaching about Phin because you wanted the job yourself."

The dogs had roused themselves again and were hovering hopefully nearby. Jubilee swore deeply.

"You know better'n that, Curt! We had that all washed out once before. I'm thinking about Crosshatch and you—and—"

"And Boone and Jesse," Ramsey

snapped. "You're still blaming me for them leaving. Well, don't waste your time," he added as Jubilee rolled the wheelbarrow up the slanted ramp onto the porch. "I can run this ranch without them."

"Expect so," Jackson replied mildly, continuing to push the improvised wheelchair on into the house. He was angry and he was guarding his tongue; saying what was on his mind could only make matters worse, as Curt was and always had been an unreasonable man. This time his bullheadedness just might cost him dearly.

"I'll be getting our supper," Jubilee said curtly and, wheeling about, he left the house and crossed the hardpack to the cookshack, with its slanted-roof dining area where the crew took their meals.

The men were already there. He could hear laughing as he drew near. Jubilee slowed, something stirring a warning inside him as he approached the structure. Stepping quietly up onto the landing that fronted the building, he paused as Durbin's voice reached him.

I'm the head honcho around here now, boys—and this ranch is the same as mine—and don't you forget it!

Someone laughed, and another voice said:

21

I'm betting you'll be owning this place before you're done!

Dan Payne stepped up behind Jubilee at that moment, and together they entered the somewhat narrow room with its long table and assemblage of chairs.

"What do you think about Curt turning over George Coe's job to Durbin?" Payne asked when they had passed Phin and the half dozen or so men gathered about him.

"Mistake, and I told him so," Jackson said, and continued on to the kitchen, where Calderone had plates of food on a tray waiting for him.

Saying nothing to the cook, Jubilee retraced his steps past the table where Durbin and the crew were now settling onto their chairs and returned to the house. He had to do something about Durbin, that was certain, but just what was unclear. He could not talk to Curt about it, and since he had no actual proof of any wrongdoing on the redhead's part, it would be useless to go to the marshal in Mesilla about it—who likely would be of little if any help anyway. And Crosshatch, thanks to Curt Ramsey's ill nature and unfriendliness, had no neighbors who might be persuaded to step in and lend a hand.

"Took you long enough!" Curt grumbled as Jubilee entered the door. "And you left me setting in this damned contraption."

"Didn't take no longer'n usual," Jackson shot back, patience with Curt running low.

Setting the tray on the table, he drew back a chair and, lifting Ramsey from the wheelbarrow, placed him on it. That done, he turned to the stove for the coffeepot. An idea had come to him—his one and only hope to save Crosshatch, he felt.

"Aim to ride into Mesilla in the morning," he said, filling Ramsey's cup with dark brew. "Anything you're wanting?"

"What're you going there for?" Curt demanded, beginning to eat. His plate was well filled with steak, fried potatoes, greens from the cook's vegetable garden, and hot biscuits.

"Just some stuff I've been needing. I'll be back afore dark."

Ramsey nodded. "Well, see to it that you are—and you best tell Calderone to fetch me my supper if you ain't here in time."

"I'll tell him," Jubilee said, "but I'll most likely be here," and, taking his plate, he poured himself a cup of coffee and sat down at the opposite side of the table.

Astride the chunky buckskin he had raised since it was a foal, Jubilee Jackson rode out of Crosshatch for Mesilla well before first light that next morning. He had but one purpose in mind: get word of the critical situation at the ranch to Boone and Jesse and urge them to come home for at least long enough to straighten out things at Crosshatch, which, according to the way Jubilee saw it, was doomed to be lost to the Ramseys forever.

He was not certain that any appeal to Boone and Jesse—assuming the messages ever reached them—would be favorably received. Between the youngest member of the family, Jesse, and the middle brother, Boone, there had never been a better feeling than toleration, and where Curt was concerned there was only a mutual hostility between the trio. Getting them all together for the benefit of the ranch had about as much chance of succeeding as riding a horse up the face of the nearby Organ Mountains, but Jackson felt he had to try.

He reached Mesilla late in the morning and went immediately to the hitch rack erected at the side of the Busy Bee Restaurant, dismounted and, tying up the buckskin which he called Buc, entered the building.

As he stepped into its warm interior, replete with the enticing odors of freshly baked bread, savory stew, and genuine coffee, he crossed to the center of the room and halted. The firm's owner, Carrie Calhoun, a widow of about his own age, had been a close friend for years.

"Anybody to home?" he called out. There were no patrons at the moment, and his deep-throated words echoed in the hushed emptiness.

"You bet there is!" a woman's voice answered, and then moments later Carrie stepped out from behind the partition that separated the kitchen from the table and chair area where patrons were served. "Saw you ride up," she added, gesturing slightly with the small pot of coffee she was holding in her hand, "and knew you'd be wanting your Arbuckles. You're looking pert."

"I ain't though," Jubilee said, pulling back two chairs from one of the tables. "Goes for you, though. By tophet, you're prettier'n ever! Always reminded me of looking at a whole hillside covered with them blue aster flowers that show up in the fall."

Carrie smiled. A large, full-bosomed woman with snow white hair and dark eyes, she still had traces of her youthful beauty.

"I know you're lying, Jubilee Jackson, but don't you ever stop! I still enjoy hearing it," she said as she filled a cup for him from the pot as well as one for herself. "You've got some trouble—that's plain as day. Curt getting harder to handle?"

Jubilee shrugged. "That's what you might call permanent, but that ain't what it is," he replied, and laid out his fears concerning Ramsey, Crosshatch, and Phin Durbin.

"Ain't no use going to the law about it. Coe tried that once before when somebody took a shot at him. This time they got him good—put a bullet in his back. He's dead."

"And Curt can't see none of it—just refuses to believe Durbin's behind any of it—the cattle rustling and Coe's murder. What about the hands that don't like Durbin? What do they think?"

"Ain't but a couple left. Others have been quitting right along because of Durbin and his bunch shoving them around. Expect Payne and Hollister'll pull out now that Curt's gone and made Phin foreman."

Carrie stared into her cup for a long

breath and then shook her head. "What are you aiming to do? You for sure can't fight Durbin and his bunch by yourself."

"I'm going to send for Boone and Jesse."

Carrie frowned, looked up. "You know where they are?"

"Nope, just got to take my chances on the letters that I'm asking you to write catching up with them."

"That's a mighty long chance, Jubilee," the woman murmured, rising and turning toward the partition. "From what I've heard, they both do a fair amount of moving around."

Carrie disappeared behind the thin wall, returned shortly with pen, a bottle of ink, and several sheets of brown paper that were combination letter and envelope.

"You have any idea where you might reach them?" she asked as she resumed her place at the table.

"Last I heard Jesse was gambling in a town called Wolf Crossing—up on the Kansas-Indian Territory border. Got it from a cowhand who worked for us a spell, quit, and then come drifting back."

"How about Boone?" Carrie asked, preparing to write. "Bounty hunters ain't known for staying put."

"Only place I can think to send the letter to him is Jimson Flats—that's up in the northern part of the territory. Been a year since I was told about him being there. Had got himself shot up some and was putting up at a hotel until he got over it."

"We could send his letter to the marshal or the sheriff, whichever they got there."

"Yeah, reckon we could, him sort of working with the law like he does, I guess it does keep him in touch with the badge-toters. We'll do whatever you think's best —and maybe it'll all be for nothing 'cause I sure ain't for certain they'll come if they do get the letter."

Carrie smiled, glanced toward the door. "You'll be surprised how thick blood can be when some outsider starts the bleeding. Now, what do you want me to write?"

Jubilee's messages were brief, identical, and to the point:

Come home. Curt hurt bad and can't work.

About to lose the ranch to a bunch of outlaws. I need your help.

Jubilee Jackson

It took only a few minutes for Carrie to

write the two letters, address the envelopes as agreed, fold and seal the sheets, and hand them to Jackson.

"Get them over to the stage depot right now and you'll catch the northbound before it pulls out. Then come back here and I'll have a meal waiting for you."

"Yes'm," Jubilee said, getting to his feet.

"And it'll be smart to talk to the stagecoach driver, tell him to pass the word along that you're needing Boone and Jesse. Somebody he'll talk to just might run into them."

"Was a time Boone was hanging around Las Vegas, then I heard he was in Dodge City—"

"What I mean. You put the word out, it maybe'll catch up with him in a roundabout way. Same goes for Jesse. Anyway, you've got nothing to lose."

Jubilee nodded and started toward the door. "That's how I see it, too, and maybe I'll get lucky," he said. "Be back right soon."

Once the letters were mailed there was nothing he could do, Jackson realized, but keep an eye on Phin Durbin and his bunch, do the best he could to protect Crosshatch interests, and wait.

4

Boone Ramsey, quickly off the sorrel gelding he was riding, hunched in the shadow of a towering pine and studied the weather-beaten old cabin on the opposite side of the creek, no more than a wagon's length in width at this point.

All around him in the later afternoon there was a stillness and, glancing up through the trees, he could see that the earlier clear summer sky was now filled with dark clouds, and the air was heavy with the smell of rain. He hoped to hell such would hold off until morning, at least. Deep in the Cimarron country on the east side of the Sangre de Cristo Mountains was no place to get caught in one of the driving thunder and lightning storms that periodically lashed the area.

The sorrel stirred nervously and lifted his long head. Ears pitched forward, his nostrils quivered in the faint breeze. Laying his broad hand on the gelding's neck, Ramsey quieted him.

"He's in there all right," Boone muttered, wrapping the sorrel's reins about the tree. "Can see two horses out back. One's Troy's. I think the other one belongs to Charley Strong. No horse there for the girl." He continued the quiet conversation with himself as was a habit with him. "Troy must have her riding double with him . . . Now, we do this right we can collect on both Troy and Charley."

The door of the cabin creaked open. Charley Strong, a squat dark man wearing two guns, stepped out into the open. He glanced up at the darkening sky and then, crossing the small clearing to a lightning-felled pine in front of the cabin, he sat down. Drawing a Jew's harp from his shirt pocket, he began to play.

Ramsey smiled. Luck was working for him. The two outlaws were no longer together in the cabin. Taking them one at a time would be much easier. Reaching down, Ramsey drew his .45 Colt revolver from its oiled holster and checked the cylinder. It turned smoothly as it always did and, except for the empty chamber the hammer rested on, was fully loaded.

A tall man for his time—a trifle over six feet—and weighing a muscular one hundred and eighty pounds, Boone Ramsey had dark hair, pale blue eyes, a full mustache, and was usually clean-shaven. Clad in brown cord pants, gray shirt, black leather vest that showed much wear, and scarred boots, he looked more to be a working cattleman than a bounty hunter. Pulling his flat crowned hat firmly down on his head, he turned his hard-cornered features to Strong. He'd best take care of Charley now, and get that part of it over with.

Dropping back into the trees and brush, Ramsey circled the cabin and drew in behind a thick clump of berry bushes. Hunkered there, he listened briefly to the twang of the outlaw's harp, and then, moving silent as smoke, gun in hand, he crossed the half dozen yards to where the man sat. An experienced veteran in such situations, Boone Ramsey wasted no time in preliminary niceties; raising the gun he was holding, he struck the outlaw a sharp blow along the side of the head.

The sound of the Jew's harp ceased abruptly, and Strong began to topple forward. Closing in quickly, Boone caught Strong, eased him backward off the rotting old tree trunk, and laid him behind it. Moving hurriedly in the event Troy Millenbow had noted the sudden cessation of the harp, Boone quickly removed the two six-guns from their decorated holsters and tossed them off into the brush. After that he took a pair of the chain-linked manacles from his pocket and coupled the outlaw's wrists together.

Again checking his .45, Ramsey moved away from the fallen tree and the unconscious Charley Strong and, approaching the cabin on its blind side, worked his way along the wall to a front corner where he could see the door. If he—

"Troy—look out! It's the goddamn law!"

At Charley Strong's warning shout Ramsey froze. The element of surprise was now lost. He could do nothing but take each moment as it came.

"Come out, Troy!" he called. "You haven't got a chance!"

"Who the hell are you?" Millenbow's voice was high and cracked.

"Name's Ramsey. Throw your gun out the door, then come out with your hands over your head."

"Ramsey! Ain't you that bounty hunter I—"

"Been called that. You coming out or am I coming in?"

"You like to take a man in hanging across his saddle, I've been told—"

"Never my choice. Prefer to take my prisoners in to the law alive. If they want to make a fight of it I'll accommodate them —up to them."

"Oh sure, I'm betting that's just how it is," Troy said in a mocking voice.

"The truth—take it or leave it. Point is, are you coming out?"

"You go to hell!" Millenbow yelled as, gun blazing, he came hurtling through the doorway.

Ramsey jerked back as bullets smashed into the corner of the cabin wall where he was standing, sending splinters and puffs of dust into the air. Dropping low, he leveled his gun at the outlaw, off balance and struggling to regain his footing.

"Give it up, Troy!" he shouted.

For an answer Millenbow, balance recovered and now racing for the safety of the trees nearby, twisted about and triggered his weapon.

In that same instant of time, and realizing that surrender was the last thing the outlaw had in mind, Ramsey fired twice in rapid succession. Millenbow seemed to freeze briefly in flight, and then plunged limply to the grassy, pine-needle-covered ground.

Boone drew himself erect slowly. A dry-

34

ness filled his mouth and throat as it always did at such moments. A man never got used to killing, no matter what folks said. Each time brought on a bleakness of the soul, a heaviness that seemed to drag at his insides and turn him cold and bloodless.

"The damned fool," he muttered. "Why did he have to do that?"

"Just like he was saying—you murdered him, shot him down cold," Charley Strong yelled. The outlaw, hands cuffed behind him, was on his feet facing Ramsey accusingly.

"It was the way he wanted it—you saw that," Boone replied. "Sit down on that log unless you want some of the same."

Where was the girl Millenbow had with him? Was she still in the cabin? Casting a side glance at Strong, now on the fallen tree as ordered, Ramsey moved up to the cabin doorway. Halting, he listened for a time and, hearing nothing, stepped quickly through the opening into the shadowy interior of the old building.

It was empty. Ramsey came about and crossed to Strong. "Where's the girl that was with you and Millenbow?"

The outlaw shrugged indifferently. "I don't know nothing about no girl."

Ramsey reached out, caught the outlaw by the front of his shirt, and jerked him roughly to his feet. "You're lying! I want the truth or—"

"She's dead—Troy shot her—"

"Dead?"

Strong nodded. "Had nothing to do with—"

"You were siding him, makes you a part of it," Boone said harshly. "But talk up. Maybe the law will go easier on you."

Another murder to add to the three charged to Troy Millenbow. Ramsey swore under his breath. "What made him kill her? From what I was told she was just a farm girl he took up with back in Kansas. What made him shoot her?"

"Hell, I don't know! What made Troy do a lot of crazy things he done? They seemed to get along real good for a couple of weeks after we left Ellsworth, then she started moaning and crying and wanting to go home."

Charley Strong paused as if reliving those days. As a gunman he was mostly bluff and show, Ramsey knew, but still he was no man to turn your back on.

"So he shot her—"

"Yep, just pulled out his iron and unloaded it into her while we was setting by the fire one night. We was talking about going to Cheyenne. She started bellyaching about wanting to go home. That's when he done it—shot her five times. Was no need for all them bullets, but Troy was kind of loco that way."

It was the nature of Millenbow, Boone thought. Ruthless, cruel, and utterly unpredictable at times. The other murders he had committed had pretty much the same impulsive insanity to them. Turning, Boone walked over to where the young outlaw lay. Picking up the man's gun, he threw it into the creek and then, grasping the dead outlaw by the heels, dragged him over to where Strong was waiting. Freeing one of the steel cuffs, Boone clamped it about Millenbow's wrist, thus assuring himself that he'd have no trouble with Charley Strong, after which he came about and went after his sorrel.

"You ain't leaving me here chained to him like this, are you?" Strong asked, voice rising with alarm.

Ramsey shook his head. "No, aim to take the both of you to the sheriff in Raton. As soon you'd be alive when we get there, but you won't be if you give me any trouble."

"Raton's a long ways from here, ain't it? Old Troy'll start stinking—"

"No more'n a long day's ride," Boone said laconically, and continued on to the sorrel.

He was back in only minutes, during which time Strong had not stirred. Tying the gelding to one of the near saplings, Boone then brought up the two horses the outlaws were riding and, removing the cuff from the dead outlaw's wrist, led Strong to a fair-size pine at the end of the cabin, encircled it with the man's arms, and restored the loose cuff to his wrist. Charley, cursing and complaining all the while, swore if he ever got loose he'd make Ramsey pay for what he was doing.

All possible interference out of the way for him insofar as Strong was concerned, Ramsey then wrapped Troy Millenbow in the small tarp that he carried, hung him across the saddle of the bay he had been riding, and anchored it securely.

He wanted no problems along the way to Raton, and the sooner he could make the journey, the better he would like it. He'd turn Millenbow over to the sheriff there —an honest man with whom he'd done business before—collect the five-hundred-dollar reward, and the one that was likely on Charley Strong's head, too, and light out for Colorado, just over the pass.

He reckoned he'd head for Boston, a town down in the southeast corner that was known to be an outlaw hangout. Maybe he could pick up another reward and add to the currency and gold eagles that were now bulging his money belt.

But if nothing worthwhile turned up there in Boston, he'd just ease on up to Denver, get himself a room at the Comstock, and lay around for a spell—maybe for the whole summer, as the days were already turning warm even there in the high country and Denver was always a nice, cool place for a man to take his ease.

5

"Your move," Jesse Ramsey said, leaning back in his chair. "Call or fold."

The saloon was in silence. Even the bartender, washing glasses in the tin tub set below the counter, paused to watch.

"Cost me a hundred dollars, that it?" the man named Cameron said thoughtfully. Only he and Ramsey were left in the game, which had begun with five players well over forty-eight hours ago.

"A hundred," Ramsey answered.

He had been winning consistently for the past ten hours, and the pile of coins and currency before him on the table represented a considerable amount of money.

In the tense hush Ramsey glanced about the saloon, his saloon, he thought with satisfaction—his for the past several years when his luck had run high and that of the previous owner, weary of an enterprise that had never come up to expectations, had run low.

Under Ramsey's ownership, and coupled with his reputation as an honest gambler, the Silver Star had prospered and become famed throughout the area as a top-grade house offering square-deal gambling, good liquor, beautiful women, dancing, and all the other diversions and needs that men coming in off the trails desired.

He had made the Silver Star a showplace after it had come into his possession—repainting, redecorating the place with pictures portraying cattle drives, hunting scenes, portraits of famous gunmen as well as lawmen, racehorses, and all else that he believed would appeal to the trade he hoped to increase.

Also, he had refurbished the second floor, where the girls lived, replacing the scarred and broken furniture and the faded and ragged carpeting with new—all imported from distant Chicago.

A new mahogany bar extended across the width of the building, with a large sparkling mirror with florid cupids and gilt roses lining its border, forming the back. New glassware, tables, chairs, portiers, gambling devices, and other companion equipment were also eventually purchased, making the Silver Star the most complete and inviting saloon in that part of the country.

Jesse never regretted that he had pulled up stakes and left Wolf Crossing, a town over on the Kansas line, when he did. It wasn't that he hadn't done well there; actually, he had something over five thousand dollars in his money belt when he'd mounted up and ridden out that summer morning with nothing more in mind than to just drift about and enjoy the fruits of his gambling.

It was just that he was tired of the dirty little trail town, tired of its people, and tired of dingy, back-room gambling. One day he hoped to have a place of his own, a real fine saloon and casino complete with all the fancy trimmings, and there in Redrock, in the Texas panhandle, his dream had finally been fulfilled.

Jesse looked up as a hand rested lightly on his shoulder. Ruby—Ruby Bellman. Slim, dark-eyed with raven's wing hair, thick brows, and full lips, she had been his woman since that first day in Redrock. He had relied upon her to keep the girls clean and attractive, and depended on her judgment in many things pertaining to that important part of the business.

Dressed now in a soft yellow dress cut low at the neck, she considered him with concern. He had been at the table for many hours and she knew he was dog tired, but she did not speak, knowing better than to interrupt him when involved in a serious game of high stakes.

"Reckon I'll call," Cameron, the last player opposing him, said, cupping his cards. He had held three and drawn two while Ramsey had stood pat with his hand. "What've you got?"

"Need to see your money first."

Cameron shrugged, dug into an inside pocket of his coat, and produced several bills. Counting out one hundred dollars, he tossed the currency onto the pile in the center of the table.

"There it is. Show me what you've got."

Jesse laid his cards face up in front of him—three kings, a deuce, and a seven.

Cameron swore, slammed his cards onto the table. "Three goddamned jacks—and they ain't worth spit!" he shouted.

Ramsey raked in the pile of coins and bills, added it to the one before him. "Three jacks—I'd say you had a call coming," he said, his voice barely audible above the rumble of conversation that had sprung to life when Cameron threw down his cards.

"But having a call don't win no hands, it seems," the cattleman said. "Mister, I ain't never seen the like of your luck. I'm beginning to wonder—"

Jesse, in the act of collecting the discard, glanced at Cameron. He studied the broad features of the man closely, speculating on the meaning of the words spoken.

"There some doubt in your mind about the way I play draw poker?" he asked quietly.

"Ain't saying that exactly—only it's mighty funny to me that every time I come up with a good hand, you have a better one."

A coolness had come over Jesse. He had never found it necessary to cheat, and having his honesty, and that of the Silver Star, challenged was far from amusing. Anger began to lift within him and then he felt the light pressure of Ruby's fingers on his shoulder calming his anger, easing the tension. A dry smile cracked his lips.

"Friend, I don't have to ring in a cold deck or do my dealing off the bottom to beat you or any man."

"Meaning I ain't much of a gambler?"

"Exactly. I could beat you with one hand tied behind my back, but if you want to take this farther we'll go outside where nobody else'll get hurt."

"Forget it, Bert," Johnson, one of the other players said, shaking his head. "You got a square deal. We all did."

The remaining men who had been in the game voiced their confirmation. One, another rancher from the Brazos River country, grinned wryly.

"Cost me a pretty penny finding out I couldn't beat him! Always heard it was hard to do. Just had to ride up here, try my luck, and see if it was true. Reckon it is."

Cameron pushed back from the table, keeping his hands in sight as he did. "I ain't claiming he's any kind of a card mechanic, was just saying his kind of luck don't seem natural."

"Well it is," Johnson said, also pushing away from the table. Coming to his feet he added, in a slightly worried tone as if fearing Cameron would carry the conversation too far, "Let's get out of here. I got some riding to do before dark."

"Same here," the man from the Brazos said. Rising, he extended his hand to Ramsey. "Was right smart of a pleasure playing cards with you—even if it did cost me."

Jesse nodded. "You're welcome in my place any time you're up this way. Can't say the same for you," he continued, looking at Cameron. "I don't want troublemakers in my place, and you're trouble."

Cameron's jaw hardened and a glint came into his eyes. Johnson half turned, laid a hand on his friend's arm.

"Whatever you're thinking, Cal, best you forget it. Ramsey's as good with that gun he carries as he is with cards."

Cameron shook off his friend's restraining fingers. He remained motionless for several moments, staring at the pile of money on the table, and then turned away.

"The hell with it," he rasped.

Tension in the Silver Star broke. Conversation once more began to fill the room as Cameron, in company with his friends, crossed to the swinging doors and stepped out into the open. Ramsey, never taking his eyes off them until they were beyond sight, picked up his winnings and glanced about for others interested in playing.

His attention came to a halt on a man just pushing through the batwings. Tall, with dark hair showing long from under his high crowned hat, features intense, he was dressed as an ordinary cowhand. The stranger paused as the dozen or so patrons in the Silver Star turned to face him.

"I'm looking for a man named Jesse Ramsey," he called out. "He around here?"

6

There wasn't much to Boston now, Boone Ramsey thought as he rode along its single, dusty street. Most of its structures were forlorn-looking empty structures abandoned to the pack rats and other varmints that had moved in. Trash lay in piles everywhere, and drifts of last winter's dead leaves had collected in drifts against the walls where the spring and summer winds had blown them.

There was only a single saloon in operation, the Paradise, where once there had been many. One general store, that of Horum Miller, was still doing business completely unopposed by any competition. The dozen or so other enterprises which had sprung up when land developers had touted and sold the area as good farming country had all gone bankrupt along with the hopes of the many who had entertained dreams of becoming successful and independent.

All had reckoned without the presence of water, a precious asset that the country around Boston lacked—and a fact that the promoters had neglected to mention to those who purchased land. Ample rainfall would irrigate their crops and fulfill their needs, those who did question the absence of a river and water wells were told.

But rainfall was as scarce as other sources. Seed died in the ground, and fruit trees hauled in from distant homelands and so carefully nurtured, withered and died. Failure was the mode of the day, and one by one the settlers packed up what was left of their belongings and moved on, bringing ruin as they did to the merchants of the town. Now the countryside was a bleak graveyard of empty, decaying houses and shacks.

Kneeing the sorrel into the hitch rack fronting the saloon, where a dozen or so other horses dozed in the summer sunlight, Ramsey drew to a halt and dismounted. Securing the gelding to the crossbar, Boone hitched at the holstered gun on his hip and, mounting the foot-high landing, entered the dimly lit building.

A half dozen men stood at the crude bar which slanted across one corner of the room. That it had seen better days was evident: the brass foot rail was partly missing, the bar itself was scarred and bullet-pocked, and only shattered bits of the mirror that once was a part of the back bar were to be seen.

Aware of the hard-eyed, suspicious glances of the men as well as the washed-out looking women in the saloon, Boone made his way to the counter. Taking his place in the line, he nodded to the bartender, a short, balding man with a black beard framing the lower half of his face.

"Whiskey—"

The bartender, studying Boone closely, nodded his head and filled a shot glass from a bottle on the bar. Conversation elsewhere in the Paradise had resumed, and two men and a woman were descending the stairway that led to the upper floor and the rooms available there.

"Don't I know you?" the bartender said, folding his arms across his chest and leaning against the back bar.

"Maybe," Ramsey replied. "Been by here once before. Was a time ago. Was another man behind the bar then."

"That would've been Ike Robertson. I got the place from him. Friends all call me Ozzie."

Boone nodded and let the introduction, half completed, drop there. He had no intention of having his name voiced.

"I'm surprised you're still doing business. Looks like everybody else but the general store man and you have moved on."

"They sure have for a fact," Ozzie agreed. "It's just me and Hebron, and a couple of hayshakers over on the slope toughing it out."

Ramsey had turned about and, elbows hooked on the edge of the bar, was glancing around in casual search for faces that belonged to wanted outlaws with a price on their head.

"You from somewheres close?" Ozzie asked.

"Nope, just passing through."

"I get a lot of that," the bartender said. "Cowboys, cattlemen, and the like on their way to Denver, and—"

Two men lounging at one of the tables looked familiar to Boone, but he couldn't be sure until he had a look at the packet of wanted posters in his saddlebags. Too, there was a couple more at the bar who would bear looking up. Boone shoved his empty glass toward the bartender.

"Once more," he said, "Have you got an empty room I can rent for the night?"

"Sure, upstairs. Woman comes with it if you want," Ozzie said. "And if you're wanting eats, the cook's got a place in the back. He'll fix you up."

Ramsey nodded, let his eyes drift slowly around the saloon again. The walls were bare except for a half dozen brewery calendars all depicting nude women in various poses. The panes of glass in the windows had all been broken out and the openings blocked with cardboard. Two large heating stoves were at opposite ends of the room, and light was provided by a single, wheel-like chandelier of oil lamps that hung in the center of the opening ceiling. Only about half of the lamps were alight, and the chimneys of those were smoked and in need of cleaning.

"You be wanting that room?" Ozzie asked, picking up the silver dollar Ramsey had laid on the counter.

"Haven't made up my mind yet," Boone replied.

Two men at a table a short distance from the bar had centered their attention on him and were having a quiet discussion of some sort. Ramsey felt a stir of caution. More than likely it had to do with his identity, one or the other, or perhaps both, believing they recognized him from somewhere. He best be on his guard; Boston was no place for a man dealing in outlaws to get careless.

Down at the opposite end of the bar an argument had broken out. Two of the patrons, both in range clothing, were having heated words about something. Anticipating excitement, nearby customers had paused and were watching expectantly.

"Ain't you Boone Ramsey?"

At the question Boone wheeled slowly. Tension built swiftly within him. Having his name mentioned in a place such as the Paradise, and in a voice that anyone reasonably close could hear, was exactly what he didn't want.

"Ain't I right?"

The man asking the questions was one of the pair he'd noticed at a table a few minutes earlier. He shrugged. "I've heard the name—"

"You're Ramsey all right!" the speaker, tall, with a full, thick mustache and wearing a dusty, faded blue suit, said. "Seen you up in Wichita about a year ago. Was when you—"

At that moment the pair engaged in arguing abandoned words and resorted to knotted fists. Both began to slug it out and then, coming together, began to sway back and forth as they locked arms about each other.

"Get him, Shorty!" someone in the circle of onlookers yelled. "Get him!"

Shorty, a heavyset individual with thick, powerful arms, immediately picked up a chair and brought it down on the head of his opponent, a slightly built but muscular cowhand.

"Damnit!" Ozzie swore as the chair splintered. "I ain't got no furniture left in this place now! Way they keep breaking things up, there soon won't be none left!"

The blow to the head had done little more than stagger Shorty's adversary. Faces contorted and shining with sweat, they came together again. Arms wrapped about one another, they began to sway back and forth, grunting and cursing as each endeavored to throw the other to the floor. The smaller man gave way, went down to one knee.

"Look out!" a voice shouted above the sounds of the scuffling.

Immediately a gun blasted, filling the room with rebounding echoes. A cloud of smoke bulged upward above the two men. Shorty staggered back, clawed at the weapon on his hip. His hand came up. A fresh wave of sound and smoke filled the room as he triggered a shot. Both men began to fall—Shorty first and then his opponent, the two of them sprawling full length on the dusty floor.

"Well, I reckon that's that," a voice drawled.

"It's been a'coming for days," another added. "Been hard feelings between old Shorty and Kansas ever since they met up."

Such shootings, Boone knew, were no novelty in a place like Boston. He had witnessed other shoot-outs in similar places many times. Ozzie, coming out from behind the bar, pushed through the crowd looking down at the two men. He beckoned to the man who had called Ramsey by name.

"Gilpin, you and a couple others grab a'hold of them stiffs and drag them out to the barn. I'll get somebody to bury them." He hesitated as Gilpin and two men moved forward reluctantly to do his bidding. "Kansas there ain't dead yet—and he's wanting to say something to you," he added, turning to Ramsey.

Boone crossed to where the man lay. Nearby Gilpin and his two helpers had taken Shorty by the arms and legs and were starting for the door.

"I—I hear somebody call you Ramsey?" Kansas asked in a faltering voice.

Boone glanced about. There was no one near. He nodded.

"Then I reckon you're the right one. I've—I've got words for you."

"You sure? My name's Boone Ramsey."

"You're him, all right—leastwise that's the name that old cowhand give me."

"Old cowhand?"

"Yeh. Said his name was Jubilee. Don't recollect the rest of his handle. Jackman, or maybe it was Jackson. You got a brother running loose out here, too? A gambler?"

54

"Yes," Boone said, frowning. "What about it—what about Jubilee?"

"Run into him in a town way down in New Mexico. Place called Mesilla. Was one day last spring. He was collaring everybody in a saloon there . . . You reckon I could have a drink?"

Boone motioned to Ozzie, who brought a glass of whiskey. Taking it from the barkeep, he held it to Kansas' lips, waited while he drank.

"I know the place," he said when the man had settled back.

"He was asking everybody in there to do him a favor. Wanted us all to keep our eyes peeled for a couple of brothers named Ramsey. Boone was one—don't recall the other'n."

"Jesse—"

"That's it," Kansas said, nodding feebly. "If we ever run into either one of you we was to say for you to come home, that somebody named Curt—"

"That's my other brother—"

"That Curt had gone and got hisself bad hurt and a bunch of hard cases had moved in and was taking over your ranch. Said he needed help."

Boone made no immediate comment, but

after a time asked, "How long ago was this?"

"Last spring—like I done said."

"That'd be three, maybe four months ago."

"Reckon it would. Maybe I come across you too late, but I done what this Jubilee asked me to do."

"I'm obliged to you," Boone said. There was no sense in taking out his anger and impatience where Curt was concerned on a dying man who only wanted to do a favor. "You know if my brother Jesse got the message, too?"

"Sure don't. Never did run into him."

"I see . . . There anything I can do for you?" Boone asked, glancing about.

Several men were standing back waiting, as if for the end. Fortunately Gilpin, the man who had recognized him, was not among them, being further occupied with carrying the lifeless body of Kansas to the barn.

"Nope—reckon I'm going under. Ain't got no sorries. Lived the way I wanted— but you sure ought to go home, help your brother. I reckon he's needing you bad —and there ain't nothing more important than kinfolk."

"I'm obliged to you, Kansas," Ramsey said again, taking the man's limp hand in a firm grasp. "You sure there's nobody you want me to get in touch with?"

There was no reply. Boone looked more closely at the cowhand. His eyes were open but a glaze now covered them. Rising, Ramsey turned to Ozzie, fully conscious of the glares, hostile and suspicious, leveled at him. His time was running out, he realized, and the sooner he got out of the Paradise, the better—if he wanted to go on living.

"I'd like to know he'll get buried proper."

The owner of the saloon nodded. "He'll get the same as all the others—a decent grave."

"I guess that's all any man can hope for," Ramsey said and, hand hanging close to his gun, hair on the back of his neck prickling, he crossed the room and returned to his horse.

7

Jesse Ramsey pushed back from the table and got to his feet slowly. The man, wearing his six-gun tied down and well forward on his hip, was a complete stranger—but that meant nothing. All too often he had known a relative to assume a grudge and take it upon himself to settle it.

Silence had fallen over the saloon. From the corner of an eye he could see that Corbett had taken up the shotgun he kept available under the bar for times when trouble arose and now had it in hand. What remained of the crowd that had been watching the game with Cameron and his friends had pulled back, and as was the way of things, keeping silent and remaining strictly neutral in the situation, whatever it was.

Turning slightly, Jesse felt the reassuring pressure of the weapon he carried—a sleek, nickle-plated, .36 caliber six-shooter hanging against his side in its shoulder holster. Motioning at Ruby to move away from the table, he faced the stranger.

"I'm Ramsey," he said coolly.

The man smiled faintly and started toward him. "Sure am glad you are! I got a letter for you."

The hush in the saloon continued as Jesse, arms folded, fingers of his right hand slightly inside his coat front, frowned. A tall, slender, clean-shaven man with pale blue eyes, dark hair, and a square-cornered face that was a trait of the Ramseys, he was wearing a tan whipcord suit, white shirt, black string tie, and fancy boots.

"A letter?"

"Yessir. I'm Ben Davidson. Work for the Overland Express Company. This letter's been chasing you around the country for months."

Ramsey's shoulders relented as tension began to drain from his body. Corbett returned the shotgun to its customary place on the shelf below the bar, and the saloon resumed its normal tenor.

Jesse took the folded, well-handled envelope from Davidson and studied the writing on its soiled surface. It had been directed to him at Wolf Crossing.

"Haven't been there for years," he said, smiling at Davidson. "Was in quite a few other places, too, before I wound up here."

"Know that now," Davidson said. "Letter's been chasing you all over the country, like I just said. The company finally run into a fellow who knew about you. Said you was running a saloon here in Redrock. Handed me the letter and told me to see that you got it."

Ramsey nodded. "Obliged to you for all your trouble," he said, and opened the folded sheet with a fingertip. "Go on over to the bar and have yourself a couple of drinks—on the house. How about something to eat?"

"A swallow of good whiskey'll do fine," Davidson said, and moved off toward the counter.

Jesse felt Ruby at his side as he unfolded the sheet of brown paper. "What is it?"

"Letter from Jubilee Jackson, an uncle of mine," Ramsey replied, reading. "He's living with my brother Curt on a ranch down in southern New Mexico territory."

"Is there trouble?"

"Looks like it. He wants me to come home. Says Curt's been hurt bad, and that a bunch of outlaws are about to take over the ranch."

Ruby's forehead puckered worriedly. She brushed at a lock of dark hair straying down over an eye. "Why can't he just call in the sheriff or the marshal—whichever there is?"

"The law doesn't count for much—leastwise it didn't when I was there. Guess it hasn't changed any, otherwise Jubilee wouldn't have written me for help."

"Curt . . . Never heard you mention him

before. You've spoken of Boone once or twice, but Curt—"

"Oldest brother. We never did get along, and I reckon I could go the rest of my life without seeing him. Unless he's changed, Boone feels the same way."

"Do you think Boone got a letter like yours?"

"Pretty sure of it, but I expect he'll be harder to find than me. He's on the move all the time—being a bounty hunter." Jesse settled down in one of the chairs surrounding the table, Ruby took the one next him.

"Then I guess you'll be going to Mesilla?"

Jesse rubbed at his jaw thoughtfully. "Can't say that I want to. Doing something for Curt's not going to be any kind of a pleasure."

"Seems to me if it's Curt's ranch it should be up to him to look out for it by himself."

Jesse looked off across the saloon to the bar, where Davidson was easing his weariness with another drink. "Well, it actually belongs to the three of us—Curt, Boone, and me. Was left to us by our pa with the word that Curt, being the oldest, was to be the head man. Wasn't too bad until he got married. Woman he took was a hellcat seven ways from breakfast. Not long after she moved in, Boone told Curt he could have his share of the place and rode off. I stood it long as I could, and then did the same."

"If you still feel that way about Curt and his wife, what makes you think you have to help him?"

"Not sure why—and maybe I don't. But Jubilee writing that letter to me sort of puts the shoe on my foot.

"My pa put his life into building up Crosshatch, that's the name of the ranch, and our cattle brand, and even if Curt and his wife are two people I don't give a damn about, it don't seem right to let a bunch of outlaws just take over the place."

Ruby looked down, shook her head. "I know you'll do what you think is right, but if you go I'll worry about you. If Curt is bad hurt it'll probably be only this Jubilee and you up against those outlaws."

"Could be the way it'll work out if Boone hasn't got a letter yet—and all of the regular hired hands have quit."

"Have you thought that it could be all over—that it's too late to do anything? That letter was written a long time ago."

Jesse nodded thoughtfully, again scrubbed

at his jaw. Outside in the street several riders passed by all, moving at a steady lope. Davidson was still at the bar, now in deep conversation with Corbett.

"Could be," Ramsey said finally, "but I've never been much of a hand to take things for granted. Something that would always bother me if I didn't go and find out for sure."

"Then you'll be leaving?"

"Next stage. Could be I'll change my mind and turn back, but right now I feel like it's something I have to do."

Ruby sighed resignedly. "You'll just have time to make the westbound. Goes through around noon."

Half turning, Jesse pulled away from the table and put an arm around the woman. "I'm leaving the place in your charge—you and Tom," he said, rising.

Ruby, smiling faintly to hide her disappointment over his decision to go, got to her feet also, and together they started for his living quarters in the rear of the building.

"We'll take care of it—and we'll all be here when you get back."

"I'll be depending on that," Ramsey said, "but if anything goes wrong just remember

63

you come first. I can always get myself another saloon."

"I was hoping you felt that way, Jesse," the woman murmured.

"Have for a long time, just somehow never could get around to saying it. Maybe when I get back we can do something about making it a permanent deal between you and me."

Ruby's dark eyes brightened. "I've been hoping to hear that, too, for a long time! Now that you've proposed to me, don't you fail to come back!"

He grinned. "I don't kill easy—but if things go wrong and I'm not back in a month, the place is yours. I'll leave a signed paper saying so."

The woman looked away. "It won't mean anything to me unless you're here—"

"I'll be back—can figure on it," Jesse said as they entered his quarters. Closing the door, he took Ruby in his arms, kissed her. "I've got too much to lose to go and get myself killed."

8

Taut, Boone Ramsey crossed the short strip of open ground to where his horse waited at the hitch rack. Casting a veiled glance behind him at the saloon doorway, he saw no one and, with the tension easing off slightly, he unwrapped the sorrel's reins, thrust a booted foot into the stirrup, and swung up into the saddle. As he settled into the hull his eyes caught movement at the side of the old building. It was Gilpin, the man who had recognized him. Standing beside him were two of his friends. Apparently they had left the saloon from a side door.

Eyeing the men coldly, every nerve attuned to the moment, Boone raised an arm slowly and took one of the slim, black stogies from the leather case in his shirt pocket, bit off the cigar's closed end, spat the waste aside, and thrust the weed between his teeth. Never removing his gaze from Gilpin and the others, he procured a match from his vest, fired it with a thumbnail and, holding the small flame to the end of the stogie, puffed it into life.

At that moment the swinging doors of the

Paradise opened and two men, carrying the body of Kansas between them, came out onto the landing. One glanced at Ramsey and then Gilpin and the pair with him. He said something to the man assisting him and then, moving across the front of the saloon, hurried toward the back.

Boone, hands lowering to where they rested on his thighs, studied Gilpin. "Something bothering you?"

Gilpin's expression did not change. After a few tight moments, he said, "Maybe."

"If it has to do with me, spit it out," Ramsey said.

Gilpin glanced at the two men with him, now standing a pace to one side. The doorway of the saloon was now filled with onlookers crowded together as they watched from behind the batwings. Word of impending trouble had spread quickly through the saloon.

Gilpin shrugged. "I reckon it'll wait—"

"The hell it will!" Ramsey snapped. "If you've got it in your head to go dogging my tracks and putting a bullet between my shoulders first chance you get, forget it! We'll settle your problem right here and now."

The two men who had lugged the body of

66

Kansas to the rear of the saloon reappeared, hurrying up the weed-littered passageway that lay between the Paradise and the vacant structure standing next to it. As they rounded the corner both slowed and then, moving carefully, crossed to the doorway and joined the cluster of men eagerly awaiting to see what promised to be a shoot-out.

Gilpin slid a side glance at his friends, and then to the front of the saloon. "You all know who this bird is?" he asked in a voice turned desperate by the difficulty he'd gotten himself in. "Called Ramsey—and he's a goddamn bounty hunter! Can bet he's come here looking for one of us."

Boone drew up slightly in his saddle, but a coolness was flowing through him, and the muscles of his long frame were relaxed and ready for instant reaction. He allowed his eyes to drift over the men on the landing and in the doorway of the saloon. He hadn't expected to take on the entire outlaw population of Boston when he rode in, but if that was the hand being dealt him, he'd have no choice but to play it out.

One sure thing: if a shoot-out developed between him at one end and Gilpin and a half dozen or more outlaws at the other, he wouldn't have to worry about making a decision as to whether he should return to Mesilla to help Curt or not. Undoubtedly they would put enough bullets into him before it was over to make it without any help on his part.

He hadn't been pleased with the message Jubilee had sent him, anyway; he had no use for his brother Curt or Elvira his wife, and for all he cared they could rot in hell. He did feel some obligation to his dead parents, and to old Jubilee, who had been like a father to him when he was growing up. However, he wasn't at all certain his debt to Jubilee Jackson was strong enough to force him to give up his present way of life.

"What's it going to be, Gilpin?" he asked quietly after a long minute had dragged by. "I've got other fish to fry. Don't aim to spend the day sitting here looking at you."

"I reckon I can fix that!" Gilpin shouted and, throwing himself to one side, he whipped out his gun.

Ramsey drew fast and sure. His bullet drove into the outlaw's chest, sent him sprawling to the ground. Taut, a grimness tightening his lips, smoke drifting lazily up from the barrel of his gun, Boone considered the crowd narrowly.

"Anybody else?"

There was no response. Someone standing in the doorway whistled softly, apparently in admiring reaction to the swiftness of Ramsey's draw, but no words were spoken. Shifting the stogie in his mouth, Boone thumbed a fresh cartridge from his gunbelt and methodically replaced the spent shell in his weapon, never for once allowing its muzzle to stray from covering the silent group of men.

"Was aiming to go north to Denver, but I reckon I'll change my mind," he said coldly. "Whatever, any of you that's fool enough to follow me will mighty quick get just what Gilpin there got."

Still holding the .45 in his hand, and keeping an eye on the outlaws in front of the saloon, Boone pulled away from the hitch rack and rode in beside an empty building on the opposite side of the street, thus effectively blocking any view of him from the Paradise. At once he put his spurs to the sorrel, rushed toward a stand of trees a hundred yards or so to the east. Reaching them, he pulled to a stop and turned his eyes toward the town. For a full quarter hour he waited and watched, and when no riders appeared he guessed he had nothing to fear from the outlaws in Boston. They wanted none of what he'd meted out to Gilpin.

Brushing aside the hollow feeling that always filled him as a result of a killing, Boone realized he was again faced with the question of what he should do—go on to Denver and take things easy for a spell as planned, or heed Jubilee Jackson's message and return to Crosshatch. To do so meant forsaking, at least for a while, his free and easy way of life and doing what he could to help Curt and Elvira out of the trouble that had descended upon them.

At the thought of his brother and his wife, Boone turned his head and spat. To give up being on the move, being a drifter who got well paid when he brought in a wanted outlaw, was the last thing he wanted to do. Folks turned up their nose at men of his kind, having an aversion to bounty hunters, although they were happy to have him bring in the killers they feared that the law was unable to apprehend.

But Boone Ramsey never wasted any thoughts on what other people thought. It was an easy, comfortable way to live, and being highly proficient with the .45 Colt he had mastered, and more or less protected by the reputation of invincibility he had earned, Boone gave little thought to the probability of one day being gunned down. He was a man who lived by instinct and intuition rather than reason, and he never considered any consequences.

Could he give it all up for even a short time? The question continued to nag at him as he swung the sorrel about and rode slowly into the grove of trees. He wondered if Jubilee had sent word to Jesse, his younger brother. Jesse was a gambler, the last he'd heard, and was running a faro table in some town in Kansas. Most likely Jubilee had, and Jesse would be thinking about helping Curt and Elvira with the same reluctance as he was.

Jesse had gotten along with Curt and his woman no better than Boone did, and while Boone and Jesse didn't always see eye to eye and had little in common, there was none of the bitterness and hostility that existed where the Curt Ramseys were concerned. They did agree on that, and years after his departure from Crosshatch, when he'd learned from a stage-coach driver that Jesse was running a game over in Dodge City, he had not been the least surprised.

Boone Ramsey drew up short. The sound

of horses moving fast reached him. Spurring the sorrel to a rise, he stood up in the stirrups and threw his glance in the direction of Boston. A hard grin pulled at his mouth. Four riders were racing away from the near-deserted settlement—headed north on the trail that led to Denver.

Boone settled back in his saddle. At least he knew where his enemies were—but what about himself? What about his own plans? What should he do about Curt and Jubilee Jackson, and Crosshatch, which, according to the word Kansas had brought, was being taken over by a bunch of outlaws?

He still owned a one-third interest in the ranch, although when he had ridden out that day he had in effect surrendered that interest to Curt, wanting nothing more to do with the place. And he sure as hell wanted nothing to do with it now—not with the ranch, not with Curt and his shrewish wife, nor with Jesse or Jubilee Jackson. He had washed his hands of the family and all its holdings, and had long ago vowed to himself that he'd never again have anything to do with any part of it. But somehow Boone couldn't convince himself that was what he really wanted to do.

What was it old Kansas had said just before he died? *There ain't nothing more important than kinfolk*. Ramsey rolled that admonition around in his mind. Thinking it over, he reckoned it could be true—or at least it should be. A family should stand together in a time of crisis, regardless of personal differences, and protect what was rightfully theirs.

At once Ramsey veered the sorrel gelding to the south. He'd answer old Jubilee's call and, while there, do his best to put up with Curt and Elvira. He'd be showing up late, but there was no help for that, and if it was outlaw trouble they were having, such would be right up his stovepipe; he'd had a lot of experience dealing with their kind, and if the situation was the same as when Jubilee talked to Kansas, he ought to be able to help. Whatever, he wouldn't stick around for long. He'd do what had to be done, assuming there was still trouble, and then ride out. And if he was too late, he'd be able to leave that much sooner.

Ramsey glanced toward the sun. It was fairly high. He could still put a few miles behind him before halting to make night camp. And then once out of the outlaw territory of Oklahoma and into New Mexico, he'd cross the Cimarron River, bear west of

Rabbit Ear Mountain and, keeping east of the Sangre de Cristos, ride for Fort Union and nearby Loma Parda. From there it would be a straight shot south to Mesilla, and Crosshatch.

9

"Ain't there no sign of Durbin yet?" Curt asked in an impatient, angry voice as he settled into his chair.

Jubilee had just finished moving him and their personal belongings from the ranch house to the old, original structure Eben Ramsey had built to house his family back when the ranch was young. In the past few years it had been used for storage.

"Ain't nobody heard nothing from him or that bunch that runs with him," Jubilee answered, glancing about.

He had matters pretty well organized, he decided. Curt and he could do their eating and sleeping in the old stone building and not be cramped—which was the reason Curt had insisted on being moved. Durbin and his crowd had simply taken over, abandoning the bunkhouse, which the crew ordinarily occupied, and taking possession of the ranch house.

"I figure it's better to have the boys close so's I can keep an eye on them," was the explanation Phin Durbin had given. "It won't make no difference."

But it had. Phin's crew was rough and rowdy, and he had let them do as they wished. When Curt objected, Durbin boldly suggested that he move out, go live in the old ranch house. Curt was furious and told Durbin in no uncertain terms that the ranch was his and demanded that Phin and the crew do as he ordered, which included their staying in the bunkhouse. Durbin had only laughed and, brushing off Ramsey's objections, continued making plans to drive the thousand head of cattle to market that Curt wanted sold.

After Phin had gone, leaving six of his men at the ranch to look after the place, matters grew worse. Durbin did exercise a certain amount of control over his crew, but now that he was absent, the men turned the ranch house into a nightmare of drinking and brawling, leaving Curt and Jubilee no choice but to move out.

"He should've been here yesterday— leastwise today," Ramsey grumbled. "And soon as he is, I want him to clear that drunken trash out of my house—get rid of them."

"You ain't never going to get rid of them—or him, Curt. Make up your mind to that."

Ramsey made no reply, no doubt seeing the truth in the older man's words. After a bit he stirred and shook his head. "Ought to be something I could do—"

"We're needing help—that's something you'd best own up to," Jubilee said, and paused. He hadn't told Curt about sending out word to the other Ramseys. "Took it on myself to mail letters to Boone and Jesse. Asked them to come home."

"You what!" Curt exploded.

"I sent for them right after you made Durbin foreman. Anybody could see what was going to happen."

"Damnit, old man—you didn't have the right to do that! They up and walked out on me, I—"

"Maybe you best say you drove them off," Jubilee cut in mildly.

"The hell! Leaving was of their own doing. I didn't tell them to go."

"You might just as well, Curt. Own up to it! You made it as hard and miserable as you could. Don't go blaming them for quitting and riding out."

Curt was silent for a long minute. A gunshot coming from the main house or somewhere near it echoed across the hardpack. It was followed by much laughter and shouting. The crew had brought in several women from one of the saloons in Mesilla and, ignoring the work that needed to be done on the ranch, much less keeping an eye on the herd, were having themselves a high old time.

"They should've stayed here," he muttered. Then, "You ever hear from them?"

Jackson moved over to the old cookstove. Removing one of the lids, he stuffed a handful of paper and dry splinters into the firebox, added several sticks of wood, and touched a match to the collection. When the wood was burning freely, he replaced the lid and set the coffeepot on its center.

"I'll have some java ready here in a couple of minutes," he said. "If you—"

"You ain't answered my question!" Curt said angrily. "Asked if you'd heard from them."

"Nope, never have. Sent the letters to where I'd last heard they was living. Been quite a time ago now. Like as not, they both had rode on."

"You ask the stagecoach people to forward the letters?"

"Sure did. Had Carrie—Miz Calhoun—put it right on the letter. Then I done some talking around the saloons. Asked all the drummers and drifters and the like to pass the word along. Figured it might get to Boone and Jesse that way if the letters never did."

Curt, still angry, shook his head. "Well, I ain't no hand to go begging for help. Not my way—"

"You ain't got no choice," Jubilee said, taking the sack of crushed coffee beans off the shelf behind the stove and dumping a handful into the now-rumbling pot. "You sure can't do nothing, and I'm too danged old to buck Durbin and his bunch."

Again Curt was silent. Finally, "When did you say you sent them letters?"

"Right after you up and turned the ranch over to Durbin. Told you then it was a mistake, that him and his bunch would steal you blind."

"I just never figured Phin would take over everything like he has. Soon as he gets back, I'm firing him."

Jubilee wagged his head dolefully. "Like I said, you ain't never going to get rid of him unless we can get help from somebody. Right now we ain't nothing but prisoners on the place and like as not we'll end up like George Coe did, with a bullet in the back."

"You reckon you might call on some of the other ranchers, tell them what we're up against, and ask them to help?"

"Already talked to most of them. All too busy, they claim. You ain't exactly been friendly with any of them, Curt. Got to remember that."

"And the law—"

"Oh, hell, you know we can't expect nothing from that kid deputy. The town ain't found a new marshal yet. Can't get nobody to take on Pete Tarbell's job."

Jubilee took a pair of tin cups from nails hammered into the wall below the shelf and set them on the table. Folding his red bandanna into a pad, he took up the pot and placed it to one side. Then with a knife he flipped back the lid, stirred down the creamy brown froth and, when it had settled, filled the cups.

"We ain't got no milk yet," Jackson said, handing a cup of the steaming, dark liquid to Curt. "Aiming to get a can from Calderone soon as I can catch him. That bunch up at the house are plain running him ragged cooking for them."

Curt dipped into the can of sugar Jubilee offered him and added several spoonfuls to his cup of brew. "Jube, you think Boone and Jesse will come?" he asked, a plaintive note in his voice.

"Hard telling," the older man replied, taking a swallow of his coffee. "Expect they're doing all right on their own, being built like they are—strong and able to stand on—"

"And I ain't!" Curt said bitterly. "I'd as soon be dead. Sure be better off."

"Hell, I didn't mean for that to sound like it did," Jubilee said hurriedly. "Only meant they could both take care of themselves, get along living without no trouble. Good boys, both of them."

"They hate my guts, both of them—that's for damn sure! Even if they ever got your letter or somebody passed the word on to them, I doubt if either one of them would show up."

"Something I sure wouldn't bet on either way," Jackson said as gunshots, several of them this time, again shattered the morning quiet. Rising, he walked to the doorway.

Two of the crew were standing on the landing at the rear of the house. Halfway across the hardpack Calderone, the cook, was legging it for the cookshack—helped along by the two drunken cowhands who were shooting into the ground behind him.

"Seems Boone and Jesse would have been here by now if they're coming," Curt said. "What's all that shooting?"

"A couple of Phin's bunch hurrahing Calderone—"

"They're going to keep on till they drive him off," Curt said angrily. "I know him. He'll just up all of a sudden and head back to Mexico some night if they don't quit it. Then they'll have to do their own cooking or find themselves a—"

"They sure better not look this way! I ain't about to start cooking for them!" Jubilee declared, refilling his cup. "They can set there and starve far as I'm concerned."

Curt shrugged. "Hope you can do what you say, but they're a mighty mean, tough bunch. Liable to try and make you do what they want."

"If it comes down to that, I'll fight the whole blamed lot of them! They can kill me, but they sure as hell can't make me do something I'm against!"

"Expect I'm getting to that point myself, Jube. Ain't much left in this life for me since Elvira died and things turning out the way they have. Once Durbin gets back I aim to straighten him out, and if I can't—well, that'll be the end of it, and me." Curt hesitated, looked off through the doorway. "You mind carrying me back out to the buckboard? I'd like to take a look around the place, see what shape the range is in, and if the cattle are needing anything. That bunch Phin left to look after things ain't paying no mind to the job at all."

Jubilee nodded. "Been wanting to do that very thing myself," he said. "Just let me get my hat—and my shotgun—and we'll get started."

10

Near dark Boone Ramsey, following a habit of periodically checking his back trail, spotted a dust cloud. It was in the direction of Boston and, studying it, he came to the conclusion that most likely it was the four riders who had left the settlement not long after he had departed, hoping to overtake and ambush him somewhere along the road to Denver.

Discovering they had been tricked, they reversed themselves, located the hoofprints of the sorrel where he had swung east, and in the interest of themselves and all other outlaws, supposedly, were now coming on fast to carry out their original plan to put him under.

Ramsey grinned tightly. He had a fair start on them, and the sorrel was a big, strong horse; he'd deal with them on his own ground and in his own time. Spurring the gelding into a lope, Boone glanced about for a landmark that would enable him to establish his location. He couldn't hope to cross No Man's Land, as the Oklahoma panhandle so favored by outlaws was known, and reach New Mexico territory by nightfall, he realized, but he should be able to make it halfway, which would put him on the Cimarron River. Such was all to his liking insofar as a plan forming in his mind was concerned.

It was still light when he reached the Cimarron. Fording its shallow depth, he continued on for a short distance and then doubled back, halted in a small grove of trees and, leaving the sorrel, made his way forward through the scanty growth to the ford. He reached there just as the outlaws rode into sight and, hunkering down behind a thick clump of juniper, he watched them ride down into the river and stop. As their horses watered Boone could hear them talking, but he was not near enough to catch all that was being said.

But he did learn what he wanted to know: the outlaws believed he had continued on south but no doubt would be forced to halt and rest his horse. They, dusty and tired, would take advantage of that fact—rest now there on the Cimarron until midnight and then press on. By so doing, and with both themselves and their horses rested and in good condition, they could overtake and surprise him, and with four of them doing the job, send bounty hunter Boone Ramsey straight to hell—a deed that would certainly earn them a vote of thanks from their *compadres*.

Boone drew back quietly into the low brush. The outlaws had turned about, were moving back up onto the riverbank, and dismounted. One, a tall, loose-jointed individual wearing a high crowned hat, gathered up the reins of the four horses and led them off to a nearby tree where he secured them.

That done, he removed saddlebags from one of the mounts and returned to the river, where a fire had been built. Dropping the leather pouches he unbuckled one, procuring a battered coffeepot and a small sack presumably containing coffee.

"Can sweeten up that Arbuckles with a little of this," one said, gesturing with a bottle of liquor he'd brought along.

Somewhere off in the closing darkness a wolf howled, the eerie sound seeming to hang in the still air for an unusually long period.

"Damnit!" one of the outlaws said feelingly. "Them things sure give me the creeps. I've heard them howl a thousand times, but it still fills me with the crawlies."

"Hell, you're sounding like some city greenhorn," one of his friends said. "Howling ain't never going to hurt you."

"Maybe not, but a man sure don't ever get used to it," a third outlaw commented.

Boone glanced up at the sky. It was darkening swiftly, and soon the stars and moon would take over. He put his attention back on the outlaws, all grouped about the fire, smoking, drinking from the bottle, and waiting for the coffee in the pot to boil. It would be easy to stage his own ambush right then and there, he thought. He could kill all four of them before they realized what was happening, but outlaws or not, that wasn't Boone Ramsey's way of doing things.

And he had no need for a plan. He knew what the outlaws intended to do, and avoiding them would be simple. Boone glanced again at the sky as he began to work his way back to the sorrel. He could use some clouds, some darkness that would enable him to move off across the flat below the river without drawing attention, but that was out. Already the land was beginning to take on a silver glow as the starlight and moonlight strengthened.

Ramsey froze. One of the outlaws had come to his feet and was looking around. He hadn't made any noise, Boone knew; he had taken extreme care to move silently, but the outlaw appeared to be staring directly at him. Taut, hand resting on the butt of his .45, Boone rode out the moments. If it came down to a shoot-out he would be in a good position to give an excellent accounting of himself. Abruptly the outlaw turned away and moved off toward the horses. Ramsey drew a deep breath and allowed his hand to leave the weapon at his hip. Remaining motionless behind a clump of false sage,

Ramsey waited until the outlaw had obtained his blanket roll from the back of his saddle and had returned to the fire, and then moved on.

No doubt each of the four outlaws would have a price on his head, and he could collect a reward on each one of them if he cared to take them in hand. But that would take time; the nearest town where there was a reward-paying marshal was the one at the foot of Raton Pass, and it was far out of the way.

Not that Boone was in any great hurry. Insofar as Crosshatch and the trouble his brother and Jubilee Jackson were in, he was already months late for heeding the old man's plea. A single-minded man who concentrated on one problem at a time, Ramsey figured that once he was finished with Crosshatch, he could head back north, visit Boston again, and throw his loop around a few of the outlaws like the ones squatting on their heels beside the Cimarron, drinking coffee-royales and bragging about their exploits. But he wasn't finished with them yet.

Silent as a summer breeze, Boone circled around the outlaws, keeping well in the shadows, until he reached their horses. Then, one by one, he untied them, and with their reins in his hand, led them back into the trees. When he reached the point where he had left the sorrel, he immediately mounted and, still leading the quartette of horses, rode quietly off into the grove.

If he were lucky he'd have fifteen or twenty minutes before the men discovered their horses were gone. That would be time enough; he needed to put only four or five miles between the outlaws and where he would turn their mounts loose to give himself a decisive lead, for a man afoot in that part of the country was a man faced with a serious problem.

He'd just not depend on that, however. He'd make it appear he was heading due east, not south, which would further ensure that he'd not be bothered by the self-appointed avengers. It came to Ramsey then that he was going to a great deal of trouble just to avoid a confrontation with the outlaws. It was something that had never occurred before. Why? He couldn't answer that, but reckoned it was some sort of inner compulsion that he did not understand —one possibly aimed at keeping him alive and well for some future confrontation. It was a sort of variation of the intuition he lived by and never ignored.

Ramsey, taking no pains to hide his trail once he was a safe distance from the enemy camp, rode steadily eastward for the better part of an hour. He heard no sounds behind him in the quiet night and guessed he'd made a clean getaway—but it was best he not press his luck too far. Accordingly, when he came to a stand of cottonwoods along the river he released the four horses, which at once fell to grazing on the thin grass.

Turning away, Ramsey cut down into the stream, no more than a dozen yards distant at this point, and allowed the sorrel to slake his thirst while he refilled his canteen. That accomplished, Boone continued on down the Cimarron for a half mile or so, finally climbing back upon the south bank of the river. He'd ride until he came to the Carrumpa and there beside that small creek make camp, he decided. Once there, he could feel that he had thrown the outlaws off his trail, and set a direct course for the next stop, Loma Parda, a small, soldier's town on the Mora River a few miles below Fort Union.

One thing had become apparent to Boone when he reached the settlement a few days later: he'd need to take on supplies and acquire a packhorse. The route he'd be following, one that took him down the sparsely inhabited areas of New Mexico territory, would enable him to avoid towns where he might encounter trouble; thus, it was necessary that he provide grub for himself and grain for the horses.

Heading immediately down Loma Parda's one street, one lined with saloons, bordellos, and a thin assortment of other establishments, Ramsey pointed for the first livery barn in sight, a squat adobe and wood structure bearing the bullet-pocked sign BILL'S STABLE.

Bill proved to be a short, husky man in faded overalls who was also a blacksmith. Turning the sorrel over to him, Boone glanced along the street, where a dozen soldiers were moving idly about along with a few of the townspeople.

"Want him looked after good," he said, pulling his rifle from the saddle boot. "He's come a long, hard way."

"What I'm in business for," Bill said with a shrug.

"I'll be needing a pack outfit—the whole works, horse, saddle, rig, and all. You got something to sell?"

Bill's interest picked up instantly. "Why,

I reckon I have. Got a buckskin that's used to packing a load. Expect he's just about what you're looking for."

"Sounds like it—if the price is right."

"Belonged to some drifter who went and got himself killed a couple of weeks ago. Can look him over if you want. Got him in the corral out back."

Ramsey followed the stableman to the rear of the barn, where a half dozen horses were standing hipshot in the afternoon sun. Entering the corral, Boone looked the buckskin over carefully. The horse was thin but showed no defects.

"How much—rig and all?"

"Well, I'll have to have seventy-five dollars—"

"A mite steep," Ramsey said, frowning. "How about fifty—in gold?"

"It's a deal," Bill said promptly, and added, "You're getting a bargain, but I'm tired of feeding him."

"Maybe. Last time I was through here horses were cheap as dirt. Like to leave in the morning at first light. Have him all ready to go along with a bill of sale."

"He'll be ready and waiting. You needing a place to sleep?"

Ramsey nodded. "Aimed to put up at one of the saloons."

"You won't get no sleep there—and you look like you could use some. Got an extra room over at my house that I rent out now and then—and my old woman's a good cook. Can eat your supper and breakfast both with us."

Boone smiled. He was hoping to remain as much out of sight as possible in Loma Parda, and avoiding the saloons and rooming houses was exactly what he'd like to do.

"Sounds fine. Where's your place?"

"Back of here a short ways. Easy walking."

"I'll take you up on your offer. Where's the nearest general store?"

"Right back up the street—the way you come in."

Ramsey turned and started for the wide door. Some kind of disturbance was taking place in front of a saloon off to his right. It was a fight in which several soldiers and civilians were involved. Bill noticed Ramsey's interest.

"Hell, that's just a squabble. Ain't nothing," he said. "You ought to see what it's like around here at night. Why, decent folks don't dare go out on the street!"

Boone shrugged. Ordinarily he would have thought nothing of the warning, would have instead gone about whatever business he had in mind despite any risk, but circumstances had altered his thinking. A peculiar contradiction possessed him; he was reluctant, almost adverse, to making the trip to Mesilla for the sake of helping his brother, yet something within him urged him to hurry on.

He was up and on his way not long after first light, with the sorrel well rested and fed and the buckskin trailing contentedly along at the end of his lead rope as only a good, well-trained packhorse will do. Equipped now with an ample stock of trail grub, an extra canteen of water, and a sack of grain for the two animals, Boone looked forward to the long ride to Mesilla with no trouble.

Keeping east of the Sangre de Cristos, Ramsey bypassed Las Vegas, a town stirring under the impetus of a new railroad, where he was well known. As the days wore on he rode steadily across the plains and through the Pedernal Hills country, skirted the vast Chupadera Mesa, the ragged, horse-crippling black lava beds to the south of it. He rested for a day at the base of nine-thousand-

foot Salinas Peak in the San Andres mountain range, and then crossed the Arenas
Blancas, a sea of glistening, white sand that
seemed endless, and halted again to rest the
horses along a small creek the name, if it
had one, he did not know.

From there he struck due west into the
Turquoise Mine country, well pleased with
the time he had made since entering the
territory at its far northeastern point. But
here progress not only slowed but came to
an abrupt stop. A half day into the area, and
just as he was nearing the crest of a hill, a
flurry of gunshots brought him up short.
Keeping below the crown of the rise, Boone
dismounted. Hunched low, he hurried to
the top, where he looked down onto a long
swale.

Ramsey swore softly. A short hundred
yards away two canvas-topped wagons were
halted side by side. Circling them, firing
steadily as they rode, was a raiding party of
half-naked Indians.

11

The pilgrims, apparently caught off guard by the Indians, had hastily drawn together for mutual support and protection. A young woman with flaming red hair flowing down her back and about her shoulders crouched in front of the seat of the near vehicle. Rifle firm in her arms, she was levering and firing steadily at the attackers. Nearby a man, evidently struck down by a bullet, was slumped to one side.

Shooting was coming from the other wagon also. Boone could see an elderly man kneeling behind its seat, his body partly hidden by the vehicle's canvas covering. He was firing rapidly, too, but like the efforts of the redheaded woman, he was having no luck at hitting any of the yelling, screeching marauders.

Something had to be done, and done quickly, or the renegades would overcome the pilgrims, already handicapped by the loss of one man. Ramsey began to draw back. At that moment the redheaded woman ceased firing. Smoke drifting above her, she began to frantically work the lever action of the weapon she was using. The gun had jammed. Probably one of the old Henry models that had a habit of failing, Boone thought as he wheeled and ran back to where his horses waited. He could hear only the reports of the one defending rifle, and those of the Indians. If he didn't act fast it would be all over for the pilgrims.

Swinging up onto the sorrel, Boone allowed the buckskin's lead rope to drop and spurred for the crest of the rise. Gun in hand, he topped the hill and started down the opposite slope at a headlong pace. The woman was still struggling with her weapon and no shots were coming from the man in the adjoining wagon—busy reloading at that moment.

Through the dust and smoke Ramsey counted seven renegades. With the sorrel plunging down the grade, he singled out one directly ahead, triggered his six-gun at the bronze shape crouched low over his pony. The Indian stiffened, rocked to one side. Sliding from his mount, he fell to the ground, limp as a rag doll.

Boone's arrival had gone unnoticed by the raiders, but now his shot drew their immediate attention. In the boiling dust they slowed uncertainly, and began to look around. Ramsey fired a second bullet at the renegade in front of him. The brave flinched, began to sway on his horse, but by clinging to the animal's mane managed not to fall. Suddenly the redheaded woman, having freed the action of her rifle, opened up. A third member of the raiding party, their yelling silenced, threw his arms about his pony's neck and swerved away.

At once the Indians began to pull off and head for a grove of trees to the south. The woman and the man in the second wagon, his weapon now loaded, continued to fire at the departing renegades, evidently finding some relief from the fear that had gripped them minutes earlier.

Ramsey pulled up beside the wagon occupied by the redheaded woman. As he dismounted she flung a grateful glance at him and then, laying her weapon aside, turned to the wounded man slumped on the seat.

"He hurt bad?" Boone asked, climbing up beside her. The buckskin had followed the sorrel down the hill and was now standing nearby in the fading dust and smoke.

"I—I don't think so," the woman replied, examining the man's wound. "Bullet hit him in the arm—the fleshy part."

"I'll take care of him."

A much older woman in a calico dress and sunbonnet, her features still drawn and reflecting the fear that had gripped her, moved from the depths of the wagon where she had apparently been posted for her safety's sake. "You best see to Zeke and Sylvie."

The girl nodded as Boone backed off and dropped to the ground. Extending a hand, he helped the redhead from the wagon. She was pretty, he noted, had blue eyes and a fair skin, and despite the man's altered shirt and pants she wore, it was apparent she had a good figure.

"I'm Zoe Tillman," she said, holding to his hand. "You came along at just the right time. We can't thank you enough."

"Glad to help," Boone said. "Hope your father's not bad hurt."

"He's my uncle," Zoe said, "and like I said, it's only an arm wound. His name's Upchurch—Gideon Upchurch. My aunt there is Sadie. Folks in the other wagon are Zeke Parrish and his wife Sylvie. She and Aunt Sadie are twins. Makes her my aunt, and him my uncle, too."

Boone smiled. "I see." Zoe's words had come out in a rush, as if she were hungry to talk to someone other than her relatives.

"I'd better see if they're all right."

Boone followed her around to the front of the other wagon. She was even more attractive than he'd thought. There was an easy grace to her, and the harrowing encounter with the renegade Indians seemed to have had little effect upon her.

"Uncle Zeke, are either of you hurt?" she called as they reached the front of the wagon.

"We're fine," a man's voice from somewhere inside the canvas-topped vehicle replied. "Sylvie's a bit shook up, but that's all . . . We're sure obliged to you, mister," he added, coming to the seat and nodding to Boone. "If you hadn't showed up when you did, I ain't sure we'd be alive now."

"Happened to be close by when I heard the shooting."

"Thank God for that," Parrish said feelingly, climbing down from the wagon. "We'd been told the Indian trouble was all over, that there weren't any more hostiles around."

"True, mostly. That was a bunch of renegades that jumped you. The tribes have outlaws among them same as we white folks do."

"And was just our luck to run into some,"

Parrish said, extending his hand. "I'm Zeke Parrish. Mind telling me who you are?"

"Boone Ramsey—"

"Want to thank you again, Mr. Ramsey," Parrish said, pumping Boone's hand vigorously. He was a tall, spare man wearing tan duck pants, a coarse gray shirt, flat-heeled boots, and a black, round crowned hat. "Zoe, is Gideon hurt bad?" he continued, turning to the girl.

"I don't think so," Zoe said. "He was shot in the arm. Aunt Sadie's taking care of him."

"Sylvie's sort of shook up. She's in the wagon laying down. All that screeching and yelling that them savages done pretty well unnerved her. You can meet her later, Mr. Ramsey—"

"Boone—"

"All right, Boone, if you're going our way."

"I'm headed west, for the town of Mesilla."

"Mesilla," Zoe murmured, eyes on Ramsey. "Is it anywhere near Las Cruces? That's where we're going."

"Could say it's right next door." Boone said. "Only a few miles apart."

"Then I reckon you know Las Cruces,"

Parrish said, glancing up. He was looking over his team for possible injuries from arrows or bullets.

"Grew up on a ranch west of there—"

"Upchurch and me, we're aiming to settle there and open a general store. Got a big St. Louis wholesaler backing us. They expect a lot of travelers to pass through the town on their way to Arizona and California."

"Ought to do right well," Ramsey said, looking off in the direction the renegades had taken. "Best you keep moving. Those braves, not sure whether they were Apaches or Comanches, will probably come back."

Parrish, finished with checking out his team and finding them unharmed, frowned. "You think they might? I always heard that once they'd been drove off—"

"Never easy to figure what a bunch like that will do. They know you're here—and I'd sure not bet on them leaving you alone."

"I understand. Trouble is, I'm not sure Gideon can drive if he's got a bad arm."

"I've been driving a little," Zoe said. "Not a whole lot, but I've spelled Uncle Gideon now and then for an hour or so."

"Both of them horses of his have got mighty hard mouths. I'm surprised you could handle them at all," Parrish said doubtfully. "How far are we from Las Cruces, Boone?"

Ramsey gazed off toward the mountains rising in the west. The Organs were a dark blue, and their numerous sharp peaks took on a church-spire appearance.

"You're about a half a day to the pass. Once through it, and coming in from this side, you'll have another long drive into Las Cruces."

Boone was vaguely aware of Zoe Tillman's eyes, frank and approving, dwelling upon him. He turned his attention to her. She smiled, unabashed at her boldness.

"Are you in a hurry to get to this Mesilla?"

"Some," Boone said, scrubbing at the stubble of beard on his chin. He had not shaved that morning, and the warmer climate of the southern region of the territory was causing him to sweat. "Leastwise, I was."

"You sure would be doing us a big favor if you'd drive Gideon's wagon," Parrish said hopefully. "And having you along if them savages come back would certainly make us all feel better."

Ramsey gave the suggestion thought. After a bit he shrugged. What the hell if he was a day or so longer in getting to Cross-hatch? He doubted it would make any great difference at this late stage, anyway. Besides, he was finding it more than just pleasant to be around Zoe Tillman.

"Be glad to join up with you," he said. "I'll tie my horses onto the back of your partner's wagon, and then we best move out. Don't figure it's smart to hang around here any longer than we have to."

"Fine!" Zoe said before Parrish could speak. Eyes shining, she added: "I'll get Uncle Gideon bedded down real comfortable, and then we'll be ready to go."

12

There were two passengers already aboard the westbound stagecoach, a rancher and a drummer, when Jesse Ramsey, now in a serviceable tan whipcord suit, dark tieless shirt, and duster, climbed aboard and took a place on the forward seat. He nodded to the two men, tucked the saddlebags containing a change of clothing in behind his booted feet, and smiled briefly.

"Fine day."

The rancher said, "It is," and fell to staring out the window. The drummer gave no response. The silence held until they reached Standish Crossing on the lower Sabine River, where the rancher disembarked without further word and a new passenger took his place—a young woman with a prim, cool manner.

She still had red hair, dark eyes, Jesse noted, and her withdrawn, quiet way bordered on hautiness. Wearing a light brown suit, white shirtwaist, and blue tie, she topped off her apparel with a sky-colored hat graced by a red feather. Not too far from the Crossing she firmly put the drummer in his place when he endeavored to press his friendship, but she did condescend to introduce herself to Ramsey, apparently deeming him the lesser of two evils with which she would be plagued during the journey ahead.

As the coach bounded and creaked and swayed on its thoroughbraces over the rutted road, she told Jesse her name was Hannah Bradley, that she was a schoolteacher and was enroute to El Paso, a town in Texas, where she had a job awaiting her. Jesse, giving her his name, listened politely to the woman, stirring only once to shift the holster on his hip to a more comfortable position. Before leaving Redrock he had strapped on his heavy .45 Colt, leaving the smaller-caliber weapon he usually carried behind, with the thought that if he faced trouble with outlaws at Crosshatch, the Colt would be a far more effective weapon.

"El Paso is right on the Mexican border, I'm told," Hannah said, continuing to carry the conversation. "Have you ever been there?"

Jesse nodded. Storm clouds were gathering in the west, he saw. They were certain to have rain by nightfall.

"Lived pretty close by. Town of Mesilla—in New Mexico."

"You don't live there now?"

"Not for several years. My brother does. Runs the family ranch."

Or he did, Jesse amended silently. He could see no reason to go into the problems Curt was facing, or had—all depending on the situation at Crosshatch at that moment.

The conversation turned to other topics in none of which the drummer participated. They changed horses at a way station called Morgan's Hollow, and again some thirty miles later at Bowie Springs. A light rain was falling as the driver pulled the coach to a halt, and with the shotgun messenger beside him, climbed down from the box.

"We stay here for the night, folks," he said, brushing at his dust-covered face with a red bandanna. "Take your suitcases with you. Lady inside will show you where you'll sleep. Expect she'll be dishing out supper in about an hour." The driver paused, glanced upward through the light shower to the steadily darkening sky. "We'll be moving out at seven sharp in the morning—if we're lucky."

The drummer, in the act of taking his gladstone bag from the guard, looked at the older man frowningly. "Lucky? What's that mean?"

"Means this here's still pretty much East Texas country and now and then we get a cloudbust that washes the roads all to hell."

The drummer shook his head. "I'm supposed to be in Tascosa by the day after tomorrow."

"You'll get there long as I have a road to drive," the jehu said.

Although a fine drizzle continued throughout the night, the coach departed on schedule and the journey west resumed. At Walls Station, the next team change, the rain ended, but when they reached the next stop it had begun again, this time in earnest. Large drops fell in what looked to be a solid wall of water, and the driver had such great difficulty in seeing that he was forced to slow the six-up to a trot.

And then at the next station, Yellow Hill, when they pulled into the yard, the hostler and the agent, yellow slickers glistening wetly in the rain, water pouring off their hat brims, hurried out to meet them.

"Pull up close to the shed, Jake," the agent called above the drumming of the rain. "Roads all washed out about five miles west of here."

Muttering curses, the driver climbed down. "When do they figure to have it fixed?"

"God only knows. That big arroyo at the foot of the bluffs has been running bank to bank all day. The cut's so deep you could lose this rig of yours in it."

Jake swore again and, turning, opened the coach door. "All out, folks. We'll be spending the night here."

"Oh, hell!" the drummer said in an exasperated voice, crowding past Jesse and Hannah Bradley. "I've got to be in Tascosa by—"

"You'll get there when the weather says you can," Jake replied, and fell back to allow him and the other passengers to step out into the steady downpour.

Jesse, laying a restraining hand on Hannah, pulled off his duster and placed it about her shoulders, drawing the upper part over her head like a hood.

"Maybe this will keep you from getting wet," he said.

Hannah smiled gratefully at him and, taking Jake's extended hand, left the coach and, avoiding the puddles of water as much as possible, hurried into the way station. Jesse followed immediately, bringing his saddlebags along with the woman's suitcase, as Jake moved the team and coach onto the rear of the place.

The drummer had settled onto a chair at one of the tables and was drinking coffee laced with whiskey as they entered. The rain had put a chill in the air, and the station agent had built a fire in the huge, rock fireplace at the end of the large room. Jesse saw Hannah, having had her room pointed out to her, cross to it and begin warming herself.

Despite the damage the weather had done to her clothing, she was still most attractive, Ramsey thought. The puffed-sleeve suit she was wearing was now damp and wrinkled despite the use of Jesse's duster; so also was her shirtwaist. The tie was gone, along with the perky little hat which left her golden blond hair to shine softly in the firelight.

"Thank you, Jesse," she said as she took her suitcase from him. "Do you think we'll have to stay here tomorrow, too? From what that man said about the rain—and the wash-out I—"

"Good chance we will," Ramsey said. Hannah's eyes were bright as they reflected the tongues of flame dancing in the fireplace, and her skin had taken on a sort of creamy glow.

Her shoulders stirred slightly. "Another day or so getting there won't matter to me. Are you in a hurry—like him?" she added, inclining her head slightly at the drummer.

"Not sure," Jesse replied. "Could be I'll be too late when I get there."

Hannah gave him a quizzical look, and then half turned about as the station agent's wife called: "I'll have some supper on the table for you in an hour or so. Meantime, you folks just make yourself to home."

"I don't understand," Hannah said, turning back to Ramsey as she sat down on the long, blanket-covered bench placed in front of the fireplace.

"Had a letter from an uncle of mine," he

said, sitting beside her, and explained the situation at Crosshatch, finishing with: "Not too happy about what he's expecting me to do. My brother and me never did get along. Could say he was the cause of me quitting ranching."

"But he's still your brother—"

"Keep telling myself that. Expect that's the reason I've come this far."

"I have no relatives left," Hannah murmured. "It must be nice to have someone."

Jesse shrugged. "Can't answer that. What I remember of Curt I don't like. Same goes pretty much for my other brother, Boone. He and I did get along, but we had nothing in common."

"Where is he now?"

"I don't know. He left the ranch a couple of years before I did. Haven't seen him since."

The drummer was steadily getting drunker. Jake entered with the Shotgun at his side, both wet to the skin. The old driver, casting an angry glance at the drummer, said something to the guard, and then both tramped heavily on to the rear and disappeared into a room which was evidently reserved for them.

"It's pleasant in here out of the rain,"

Hannah said, looking about at the walls decorated with the heads of deer, calendars, and photographic prints taken from magazines. Several lamps bracketed to the walls added to the glow of the fireplace, and the room was filled with the tantalizing odors of cooking food.

"Will your room be near mine?" Hannah asked, again nodding at the drummer.

"I'll see that it is," Jesse said. "If you need me just yell."

But nothing occurred during the long night, and next morning they all boarded the stage and continued the journey west. But it was short-lived. The arroyo was running as wild and deep as ever, and they were forced to turn back to the way station, where they idled away another day and night.

On the following morning, however, word came as they were eating a breakfast of meat, potatoes, hot biscuits, and coffee that the arroyo had run itself out during the night, and that a team of draft horses were there waiting to hook on to the six-up and help them cross the treacherous, muddy wash.

Filled with hope, the passengers loaded up and made the trip to the arroyo. The team of big grays hooked on to the tongue of the coach, and with considerable effort because of the hub deep clay mud that sucked and clung to the iron-tired wheels, eventually managed to pull the vehicle across.

They rolled into Tascosa shortly after dark, dead tired and hungry. The drummer disappeared as soon as he was handed down his luggage, and Hannah, eating a quick supper of beef stew and light bread, made her excuses and went on to bed, too near complete exhaustion to join Jesse in the hotel's lobby and casino.

A new driver and shotgun guard, Tom Donovan and Kelly Adams, took over the coach along with a fresh team that next morning, and they were once more on their way. This time Hannah, refreshed and fetching in her suit and shirtwaist, which she had managed somehow to clean and iron, and Jesse, also much improved after a night's respite, were the only passengers. The day was clear and sunny after the downpour, with larks springing up into the clear air on both sides of the road at every hand as the big coach thundered by.

Apache Wells, Rowena, Devil's Canyon, Sage Flats, and Flat Rock way stations were all reached and the team changes made without trouble, after which the stage whirled on. During the long hours Jesse and Hannah Bradley became better acquainted, she telling him of her life back east, he remembering the days at Crosshatch before dissension broke up the family.

"It wasn't long after Pa died, and Curt took over running the ranch, that things sort of went to pieces," he said. "It wasn't that we resented Pa leaving Curt in charge. He's the oldest, and it's only natural that—"

A rattle of gunshots sounded above the popping and creaking of the stage. A shadow hurtled past the window—the body of the shotgun guard.

"Get down on the floor!" Jesse shouted. "It's a holdup!"

Pushing the woman into the space between the seats, Ramsey drew his gun and moved up close to the window. The stage was slowing, and from the way the lines were sagging, Jesse knew that Tom Donovan had been hit, too.

"Pull up!" a harsh voice yelled. "Pull up, old man!"

Brake shoes began to screech against the iron tires of the wheels, and the Concord rolled slowly to a stop.

"Everybody out! And you, driver, throw

down that mail box unless you want what your Shotgun got!"

The door was suddenly yanked open. A squat, bearded man in a dirty gray shirt and stained black britches, gun in hand, peered in. A wide grin split his thick-lipped mouth. He half turned to the rest of the holdup party—four more men looking much the same as he.

"Well, what do you know!" he shouted. "We ain't only got us a cash box but we got us a pretty little gal, too—the one we seen in that saloon in Wichita!"

"You're sure as hell right!" a second outlaw said, crowding up for a look. "Well, she was just plain too good for us up there. Reckon now we'll see who's too good for who!"

"Drop that iron you're holding, mister," the first man said, "and come on out of there," he added, waggling his weapon to emphasize his command.

Jesse glanced at Hannah. The words the outlaw had spoken were lodged in his mind along with a fear for her. He faced the outlaw, and shook his head.

"All right, but leave the woman alone. She—"

"Now, who the goddamn hell do you

think you are? This here little fandango's ours!" the outlaw snarled and triggered his weapon.

Ramsey felt the shocking impact of the bullet just above his left temple. Brilliant lights flashed in his eyes, and then a flow of blackness engulfed him.

13

Jesse Ramsey fought his way slowly back to consciousness. He became aware of the afternoon light, and then of a stickiness on the side of his head, and that he was lying partly under the stagecoach. Pain was hammering steadily at him, and for several minutes he remained motionless, allowing his mind to clear gradually, while an inner caution directing him not to stir until he was certain he was alone took over.

He could neither hear nor see anyone. There was only the brilliant blue sky bending over him and the distant cooing of a dove. Rolling over he sat up, a recollection of what had taken place flooding into his mind. The outlaws . . . The shooting, and the girl, Hannah Bradley—where was she?

She was gone. The outlaws had taken her

along with whatever it was they had gotten from the strongbox. Jesse saw Donavan then. The driver was sitting slumped against a front wheel of the coach. Picking up his gun, Ramsey got unsteadily to his feet and made his way to the older man. He appeared dead, but after a brief examination Ramsey saw that he was only wounded and unconscious. Moving about more rapidly now as his body began to function at full capacity, Jesse took the canteen of water from the floor of the box and, squatting beside Donovan, poured a quantity of it onto the driver's face. Tom stirred slightly, and after a bit his eyes fluttered open.

"What—what the hell—"

"Just sit there a minute," Jesse said, wetting his bandanna and mopping at the drying blood on the side of his face. "You've been shot, and then I guess you fell off the coach. Not sure how bad you're hurt."

"Bad enough, I reckon. Can't hardly breathe—or move. Where's Kelly?"

Ramsey glanced back up the road to where the Shotgun's body lay. "Expect he's dead. I'll take a look."

There was no help for Adams. Ramsey hurriedly picked up the guard's slight figure and carried it back to the stage. Placing it inside, he turned to Donovan. The old driver had pulled open his shirt and was gingerly fingering a slowly bleeding bullet wound in his side.

"We best doctor you up next," Jesse said. "Get that shirt off."

While Donovan removed the blood-soaked garment, hidden from sight earlier by the jacket he was wearing, Ramsey took a clean shirt from his saddlebags and ripped it into strips. Forming a pad with one, he pressed it against the puckered, seeping bullet hole and then bound it in place with a bandage encircling the older man's waist.

"That'll hold you till I get back," Ramsey said, coming hurriedly to his feet. "Those outlaws took off with Hannah—the woman passenger. I've got to go after her."

"You do that—and don't fret none about me. I'll make it to the next station. Only about eight or nine miles." Donovan drew himself erect slowly. "You'll be needing a horse. Take the off-leader. He'll be easier to handle."

Jesse wheeled and hurried to the team, and quickly freed the bay horse Donovan had mentioned—using his knife to slash the harness that could not be easily removed. Leaving only the bridle with a short length

117

of reins, he swung up onto the animal's broad back. The horse, not accustomed to such, began to shy but after a moment settled down.

The direction the outlaws had taken, secure in their belief they had left no survivors, was plain. The tracks of their horses led east toward a grove of trees a mile or so in the distance. Once he had determined the point for which they had struck, Jesse wasted no time on the tracks but put his horse to a steady lope for the trees.

What was in the strongbox was of no interest to him; what could happen to Hannah Bradley was. He recalled suddenly what one of the outlaws had said about her: . . . *we got us a pretty little gal, too—the one we seen in that saloon in Wichita;* the man who had jerked open the door had yelled. After which one of the others had added: . . . *she was just plain too good for us up there. Reckon now we'll see who's too good for who!*

The words now hit Jesse Ramsey with solid force. Hannah had lied about her past. She was no schoolteacher but a saloon girl, one evidently trying to break away and change her life. Jesse shrugged as he stared ahead. Hell, he couldn't fault her for wanting to better herself—he only wished she hadn't lied to him about it.

The horse veered abruptly as a jackrabbit exploded from a clump of false sage with a thump of his hind legs. Jesse clawed at the bay's mane to keep from being thrown. It had been years since he'd ridden bareback, but like so many things in life, once mastered it was something a man never forgot. Straightening up, and taking a firm grasp of the reins, he clamped his legs tight to the bay's body and rushed on.

He saw smoke when he was a short quarter mile from the grove. If it was coming from a fire the outlaws had built, he was running in luck—and reasoning it out, he reckoned it most likely was so. Fearing no immediate pursuit, the outlaws would stop, split up the cash, and possibly even make night camp. Ramsey's jaw hardened as that thought came to him, and what it would mean to Hannah Bradley. Crouching lower over the big horse's back, he urged him to a faster pace.

Ramsey gained the grove, slowed. He couldn't take a chance on the sound of the bay's running being heard. Too, he no longer had the plume of smoke to guide him; he would have to locate the fire, hopefully that of the outlaws, by smell and by continuing on in the general direction established in his mind by the smoke plume. Abruptly Jesse pulled up short. Voices came to him through the trees and brush, seemingly only yards ahead. Quickly dismounting, he tied the bay to a tree and began to make his way toward the sound.

The voices grew louder, more boisterous. He was certain it was the five outlaws, but as yet he had seen no one. And then as he came up to a stand of thick brush the fire was suddenly in partial view just beyond. Instantly Jesse dropped to his knees. He listened briefly to the raucous talking and laughing in the small clearing, but could get no clear view. Drawing his gun, Ramsey circled through the waist-high weeds and bushes to a point where his vision was no longer impeded.

All doubt as to whether it was the outlaws vanished. They were squatting about the fire, in which a blackened coffeepot had been placed. Evidently they had already divided the money taken from the strongbox, as two of the men were fingering packets of currency while another toyed with several gold coins.

Where was Hannah?

Throat tight, Jesse raised himself slightly for a better look into the small, open area. Relief rushed through him. The woman was directly opposite, partly hidden by shadows. The outlaws hadn't felt it necessary to gag her, but her hands were tied behind her back and both ankles were lashed together. Helpless, she lay with a shoulder resting against the trunk of a tree.

"Who's getting the gal first?" one of the outlaws asked, taking a swallow from the bottle of whiskey he was holding. He passed the liquor on to the man next to him. "I seen her first back there. Seems she ought to be mine."

Hannah was in the line of fire if he had to shoot, Jesse realized. He would have to circle around the clearing, hope he could do so unseen until he reached a point where Hannah would no longer be in danger. If he could make it to the tree that was directly behind her, he might be able to free her without having a shoot-out.

"That argument ain't no good," said the outlaw sitting directly across from the first man. "We all seen her just about the same time you did. Why, back in Wichita it was me that—"

"Maybe so, but was me that rigged up

this little fandango. Way I figure it, she's mine."

"Why'nt we draw straws? Man who gets the short one, gets her."

There was silence for several moments, during which Ramsey was working his way around the clearing toward Hannah, and then two of the outlaws nodded. A third followed, and finally the fourth.

"Sounds all right to me," the last of the party said. "I'll get some of that bunch grass."

"What'll we do with her when we're done?"

The man who had opened the coach door gestured indifferently as he helped himself to a drink. "Sure can't let her run loose —she'll go blabbing to the first lawdog she can get to about us and them killings back there on the road."

"Kind of a waste, Henry. I'd sort of like to have her around—leastwise for a spell."

"Best you forget that, Pearly—"

"Here's the straws," the outlaw who had collected several blades of stiff grass cut in. Arranging them fanlike in his hand, he held them out for the others to make their choice.

Jesse stopped. He was still a considerable distance from Hannah, and was realizing he'd not reach her in time to release her before the outlaws turned their attention her way.

"By God—she's mine!" the outlaw called Henry yelled, coming to his feet. Wheeling, he crossed to where Hannah lay. "Girlie, you and me are sure going to have us a good time!"

"Strip her off—make her dance for us first," one of the men at the fire called, as Hannah began to struggle against her bonds.

"Nope—later maybe," Henry replied and jerked the woman to her feet. Grinning, he grasped the front of her shirtwaist and with a jerk ripped it open. Hannah screamed, endeavored to pull away. Henry cursed and slapped her hard across the face.

Jesse Ramsey, anger roaring through him, rose to his full height. Leveling his gun, he dropped Henry with a bullet in the head. As the report of the weapon echoed through the fading day, the startled outlaws leaped to their feet clawing for the guns holstered on their hips. Cool, with no feeling, Ramsey drove a bullet into another of the renegades.

The three remaining outlaws, off guard and unnerved by the quick death of two of their party, broke and ran toward their horses waiting off to one side. Gun ready, Ramsey crossed quickly to Hannah and, keeping an eye on the fleeing outlaws, slashed the rawhide cords that bound her hands and feet.

Hannah murmured her thanks and smiled wryly. A strong woman, she did not break down at the conclusion of the ordeal to which she had been subjected, but was taking it all in stride.

"I'm sorry I lied to you about myself," she said. "At the time it seemed best."

"Forget it," Ramsey said. "Nothing's changed." He turned his head and looked off in the direction the outlaws had fled. "Let's get out of here. We'll take the two horses the outlaws left—their friends won't be needing them—and ride to the next way station. It's only a few miles, according to the stage driver."

"Do you think they—those out-laws—will come back?"

"Can just about bet on it. Just need to screw up their nerve a little—and it's not long till dark."

Hannah shuddered, giving way for the first time to the fear and horror that had gripped her. "I—I'll always be grateful to you for coming after me. I thought they'd killed you like they had the shotgun and the driver."

"Just grazed me, and I think Donovan'll make it. Got shot in the side, and he hit his head pretty hard when he fell from the coach. The Shotgun wasn't so lucky," Ramsey said, leading the way to where the outlaws had tethered their mounts. The pair belonging to the dead men shied nervously as Jesse and the woman approached.

Freeing one, Ramsey helped Hannah up into the saddle and then mounted the other once its lines were untied. "I'll send somebody back for the horse I rode, and for the bodies of the dead men when we get to the way station," he said, glancing about.

"They don't deserve any consideration! Animals, that's all they are," Hannah said bitterly.

Jesse nodded. "Expect you're right, but somebody'll be coming for the horse, and they might as well load up the two stiffs and haul them in for burying. Anyway, somebody just might collect a reward on them . . . You planning to go on to El Paso?" he added as they rode off into the trees.

Hannah nodded. "Certainly. Nobody down there knows anything about me—"

"That's no guarantee you won't run into somebody like this bunch who saw you in Wichita."

"I know—and Wichita's not the only place. There are a half dozen other towns," the woman said heavily. She smiled. "But there's nothing I can do about it—but hope."

Jesse said, "True. And it's the best way to look at it. Thing to remember is that most everybody has something in their past they'd like to forget, and most have made a fresh start at a new life. You'll be doing the same."

Hannah smiled faintly. Without the little hat she had worn, her red hair glistened brightly in the afternoon sunlight. "Yes, I guess I will."

"Folks are always looking for a place where they won't have to be afraid, where they can live in peace. Only way they can find it is to forget the past and keep right on living in the present and for the future."

Hannah looked at Jesse curiously. "You sound as if you've gone through something like this."

"Just about, but in a different way. Problems with my family."

"I see. If things aren't right with you and

126

them, is there a chance you could come on to El Paso with me?"

Jesse was silent for a long minute. Color was beginning to spray up into the sky from the western horizon, and off to their left a flock of scrub jays were quarreling noisily in the trees as they prepared to settle down for the night.

"No, I'm afraid not. Got to see what I can do about the trouble at the ranch—not that I give a damn. It's just that I somehow feel that I don't have a choice."

"But when that's all over—"

Ramsey shook his head. The last thing he wanted to do was hurt Hannah Bradley. "Need to think about that," he said, and pointed to smoke rising above the trees ahead. "That'll be the way station. I reckon we're just about there."

14

"Get me over to the house!"

Curt Ramsey's voice was harsh and demanding. Jubilee, putting a half dozen potatoes on the stove to boil, turned. "Now, just what are you aiming to do?"

"I want to see Durbin before he leaves."

Phin had returned from the cattle drive late that previous day. Curt had waited impatiently for him to report—and explain why he had sold all three thousand head of Crosshatch stock instead of just the one thousand Ramsey had intended.

"What am I aiming to do?" Curt echoed, squirming in his chair. "I want to know what Phin's been up to, and what he's done with the money he got for selling off my stock—that's what I aim to do! And there's some questions I want answered . . . Come on, come on! He'll be riding off if you don't get a move on."

Jubilee pushed the kettle of potatoes and water to the back of the stove and, coming about, pushed the wheelbarrow over to where Curt was sitting. Lifting the rancher, the older man placed him in the improvised wheelchair.

"Give me my gun," Curt said, pointing to the holstered weapon hanging from a peg in the wall.

Jackson shook his head. "Nope, I sure ain't going to do that, Curt. You go over there and start fussing and fuming with Phin with a gun in your lap and you'll get yourself killed sure'n hell!"

Curt swore deeply. "Goddamnit, I got to

do something! Can't keep on setting around and let Phin and his bunch steal everything I've got."

"Know how you feel, and I'm still hoping something'll turn up before he gets away with everything—the boys'll come riding in, or we'll get a lawman in Mesilla."

"Hell, Boone and Jesse ain't coming," Curt said, brushing at the sweat on his forehead. "They'd a'been here by now if they were."

"I just don't know if—"

"Well, I know one thing!" Ramsey cut in. "If it was Pa in the fix I'm in, he'd take up a rifle and blow that damn Phin Durbin's head off—and that just what I ought to do!"

"And then find yourself listening to some judge tell you that you was about to be the main attraction at a necktie party—if two or three of Durbin's bunch didn't fill you full of lead first."

Curt cursed again, wagged his head. "I ain't never backed away from anything. It sure galls me to be doing it now, specially when I own the place . . . Come on, let's go."

Jubilee took up the wheelbarrow's handles and started toward the door. "You think Phin knows you're onto him—about him selling off the whole herd, I mean?"

"Can't be sure. Can bet he didn't figure I'd go riding about on the range, and finding out what he'd done. A cripple ain't supposed to do that."

Jackson wheeled Ramsey on out onto the landing of the old house, halted. Durbin and three of his hard cases were walking slowly across the yard.

"Phin!" Curt shouted. "I want to talk to you."

Durbin hesitated, said something aside to the men with him, and then all four came about and sauntered indolently over to where Curt and Jubilee were waiting.

"Yeah, Mr. Ramsey?" Phin said in a mocking tone.

"You got back from the drive yesterday. I expected to hear from you then."

"Was a mite busy—and this is a big ranch I'm—"

"You sold off all my herd—I know that. And you've got a draft for around fifty thousand dollars. I—"

"Who told you that?"

"Never mind who. Happens I still have a few friends around." Ramsey's features were flushed with anger, and his lips trembled. "I want that draft."

Durbin shrugged. "Sure. Had the cattle buyer make out the draft for all but a thousand dollars. Needed cash to pay off the crew and for other expenses."

"All right, you spent a thousand. I want the draft that covers the balance."

"It won't do you no good. It's made out to me."

"You! Goddamn you, Phin Durbin, don't you try—"

Two of the men with the foreman stiffened and came about to where they faced Ramsey squarely. Jubilee hurriedly raised his hand.

"Easy now. Curt ain't armed. I ain't either. Just you forget about that iron you're carrying."

In the tense hush that had fallen over the hardpack, Calderone could be heard banging pans about in the kitchen as he made ready for the next meal. High overhead in the warm sky buzzards were circling, their interest on something south of the ranch buildings.

"No, there ain't no need for gunplay," Durbin said with a wave of his hand. "You'll get your money, Mr. Ramsey. I figure on going to town—to Las Cruces—today and getting the draft cashed at the bank."

One of the men with Durbin laughed. Jubilee shook his head. "You've already cashed that draft, Phin. We was told that—"

Durbin's features hardened. "I don't give a damn what you've been told—or who told it to you! Now, you'll get your money, Mr. Ramsey, when I get around to giving it to you! I'm real busy now. Meantime, it's best you don't bother me. We sure don't want another accident around here."

"Why, you—" Ramsey exploded. "I—"

But Phin Durbin had abruptly spun on a heel, and with his three shadows following him, continued on to the ranch house.

Curt slumped wearily into the padded box of the wheelbarrow as Jubilee swung it about. "He's figuring on keeping my money, Jube—every last dollar of it," he said helplessly. "Probably'll ride out some day or night, and leave me flat busted—and I can't stop him."

"You want me to ride to El Paso and see if I can get the sheriff there, or maybe a Texas Ranger, to step in?"

"Won't be no use. They'd tell you that

they can't do nothing about something going on in New Mexico. Out of their jurisdiction, they'd say, and they'd be right . . . Just let me set out here a bit, Jube," Ramsey continued, his voice low and despairing. "Want to do a mite of thinking."

"Sure," the older man said, turning the wheelbarrow slightly to where the sun would not be on Ramsey. "I'll see to heating up the coffee."

His one salvation was for Boone and Jesse to show up and take charge, Curt thought, and that was a farfetched, likely-not-to-be hope. He'd driven them off, made them feel unwelcome and unwanted, thus severing the family connection. If he hadn't been so hard on them, or let Elvira have a say in running the ranch, Boone and Jesse would probably be there now—and Phin Durbin most likely would never have been heard of. But thanks to him, that wasn't the way of it.

Curt let his gaze drift over the hardpack. Small dust devils were spinning across its packed surface as a vagrant breeze slipped in from the flats to the south. Old Calderone was still rattling his pans in the cookshack, and the buzzards had drifted away, leaving the bright blue sky uncluttered. In the wire pen he'd built for Elvira's chickens, sparrows and several scrub jays were vying for scraps of food, and overriding it all came a burst of laughter followed by loud talking from the main house where, he supposed, Phin and his crowd were having a card game. Curt sighed deeply.

I done the best I could, Pa, but I reckon it wasn't good enough.

The words formed involuntarily in Ramsey's mind and hung there, motionless and accusing. He had done the best he could according to the way he'd seen it—but it looked now as if he'd been wrong. He'd managed, thanks to his poor judgment in picking a wife, to drive Jesse and Boone away. Pa should have left the ranch in the hands of Boone, or maybe even Jesse, who wasn't much more than a kid at the time but who likely would have done a better job running Crosshatch than he.

But, hell—there wasn't any sense in wallowing around in regret and thinking of what might have been. A man was a damn fool to look backward and sweat and growl over the things he'd done wrong. There wasn't one thing he could do about it unless the chance to right the wrongs he'd committed presented itself. But such never happened. He could forget about that ever coming to pass.

Months had elapsed since Jubilee had put out word to Jesse and Boone asking them to come home—to help—and not one word had been heard from them, much less either of them putting in an appearance. There was but one answer, Curt decided; he'd gotten himself into this fix, and now, crippled and laid up or not, he'd set things straight himself—and doing that meant putting a rifle bullet in Phin Durbin's head regardless of the consequences.

15

"That smoke yonder," Boone Ramsey said, pointing to a thin smudge of dark gray beyond the bobbing heads of the plodding horses, "is Las Cruces. Just a little ways past it is Mesilla."

They had left the vast flat with its glistening white sand, towering San Agustin Peak, and the multispired range of mountains called the Organs behind, and now were moving at a good pace along the grassy road paralleling the Rio Grande.

"Ought to get there about the middle of the afternoon," he finished.

Zoe, having discarded her rough, men's clothing for a skirt and blouse that set off her small waist and ample bosom to good effect, stirred wearily on the seat beside him.

"I'm glad," she said above the rattle of the wagon and clinking of the trace chains, "but I'm sad, too."

They had become very well acquainted since meeting, and now Boone was feeling a twinge of regret at the realization they would be parting before the day was over.

"Reckon it's the same with me."

He had never met a woman like Zoe Tillman. Not only was she beautiful, but she was equally capable at cooking, handling a rifle, and driving a team and wagon. At times she looked soft and delicate, the beauty of her face seeming to glow, and then some sort of emergency involving her aunts or uncles would present itself and at once an inner strength would come to the fore demonstrating a cool ability that Boone never suspected a woman could possess.

"This ranch you spoke of," Zoe continued, "do you really have to go there?"

Boone brushed at the sweat on his face. "Not happy about the idea."

"Is it your ranch?"

"Guess I'm sort of a partner. My brother Curt has been running it for years. I walked out on it—him. Told him he could have my share."

"Then why are you going back?"

Off to their right a dozen or so ducks veered sharply from their skyway course and slanted down to rest on the sluggishly moving water of the river. Near where they had landed several long-legged cranes were stalking majestically about in the shallows, and on downstream a dog was barking.

"Got word from a drifter up Colorado way that Curt was in bad trouble and was asking for help," Ramsey said, and told Zoe of Jubilee Jackson's message. Finished, he shrugged.

"Been asking myself ever since I headed south why I am doing it. I've got no use for Curt and he don't have any use for me—and I sure don't owe him anything."

"He's kin," Gideon Upchurch, resting on a pallet immediately behind the seat in the wagon, said. "That's why you're doing it. It's natural. The same blood runs through both of you."

Ramsey shook his head doubtfully. "Not sure that has anything to do with it in my case."

"It has everything to do with it—with living, especially out in this part of the country, where folks are mostly on their own. Families have to stand together, else they'll mighty soon lose out."

Boone made no answer, and after a few moments Zoe laid her hand on his arm. "Maybe Uncle Gideon doesn't understand," she murmured. "Maybe there's more to it than he thinks."

Ramsey nodded, thinking back to the years, to the times of bitterness and near hatred. "There is—and I'd as soon not rake it up. Too many scars."

"And you're thinking that's just what will happen if you see your brother again—"

"Just how I see it, and it's been gnawing at me ever since I left Colorado. I've got another brother mixed up in it, too—Jesse. We both pulled out, let Curt have the place rather than put up with him and the woman he'd married. I don't know if Jesse got the same message I did or not. Could be it never reached him."

"Who sent word to you by that drifter —Curt?"

"No, he's too proud for that. It came from an uncle of mine, Jubilee Jackson. Always lived with us—sort of raised us boys."

"You saying there's three of you brothers, and an uncle, that it?" Gideon said.

"Yes. Pa died years ago, leaving Crosshatch—that's the name of the ranch—to us boys, but putting Curt in charge since he's the oldest . . . It's going to be a mite hard helping him no matter what the trouble is."

"You know what the trouble is?" Gideon asked.

"Something about a bunch of outlaws taking over the place. Seems Curt got himself hurt a time back and has to depend on hired hands to keep things going."

"Crosshatch—that's a strange name for a ranch," Zoe said.

"Pa's doing. Don't know where he got it—or why."

"A word that stuck in his mind from somewhere, I expect," Upchurch said. Then, "You hate this brother—Curt?"

Boone felt Zoe's fingers tighten on his arm. Her uncle was delving far too deeply into his personal life, she realized, and was letting him know that she'd put an end to it if he so desired. But such was unnecessary; as well get it out in the open—and it did

make him feel better to talk about it to someone.

"Reckon I'd best admit it—hate's the
word. Like I've said, I've got no use for him
or for the woman he married. Could go the
rest of my life without ever seeing or even
thinking about either one of them."

"But he's blood kin—there ain't no getting around that, and blood kin should always stand by each other. If they don't this
country—the whole world, in fact—will fall
apart. Expect it's the same out here as it is
back where we came from. A man fights
like the devil to get something in life, then
he has to fight to keep it. That's where kin
standing together comes in. Ain't that true
out here?"

Ramsey stirred, slapped the rumps of the
horses with the slack in the lines. Mesilla
was getting near, and he was finding the
conversation with Gideon Upchurch making him uncomfortable. Twisting about, he
looked back to the Parrish wagon. It was
not far behind.

"Expect you're right," he said.

"It's probably even more so," Upchurch
continued. "From what I've been told, the
law ain't much and folks can't depend on it

140

for protection, mostly because lawmen are scarce. Ain't that true also?"

Boone nodded. "Man sort of has to look out for himself."

"Just what I've been told. Understand you're some kind of a lawman, a—a—"

"Bounty hunter, that what you're trying to say?"

"Yes, that's it. You go out and get the outlaws who have rewards on their heads—"

Ramsey made no comment. Mesilla, and Las Cruces, were not far ahead. They would reach the latter settlement first, and he'd deliver Zoe and the Upchurches and the Parrishes to the hotel in Cruces, pausing long enough at the saloon next to the hostelry to have a couple of drinks, and then ride on to the ranch. It had been a long, hard, and dusty drive, and his throat was parched. Besides, it wouldn't hurt to fortify himself if he planned to go through with meeting Curt and his wife.

"You like that kind of work?" Gideon asked.

"Good a job as any, I suppose."

"But isn't it terribly dangerous?" Sadie Upchurch, who had been listening in silence, wondered as the wagon rolled steadily on. "I would think that outlaws, being so desperate as they usually are, would be on the watch for you—actually try to kill you if they got the chance."

"That's the trick—don't ever give them a chance."

"Meaning you kill them before they can kill you, is that it?" the older woman continued.

"Yes, ma'am, that's how it is. But they get a choice. If they want to use their guns, or come along willingly—it's up to them."

Mrs. Upchurch sniffed audibly. Gideon muttered something inaudible—no doubt in disapproval. Boone glanced at Zoe. They had reached the fringe of Las Cruces and were entering its main street.

"Sounds like the way I make a living's not too popular with your folks," he murmured with a tight grin.

Zoe smiled. "They're used to living in a city. What you do sounds exciting—and it's all right with me."

Boone studied the woman's calm, lovely face quietly. He should have known she would feel that way; no matter what her man did she would go along with him on it—even to the point of whether it was within the law or not. He glanced ahead.

The hotel where the two parties intended to stay temporarily was just down the street.

"I'd kind of like to see you again after I've got this business at the ranch straightened out," he said.

"Then you're going to see Curt—"

Ramsey's shoulders lifted and fell. "Still not too certain—but I've come this far."

"I think you should—and as for seeing me, I'd like that."

"Can figure on it then," Boone said and turned into the driveway running alongside the hotel. "I'll help you unload and stable the horses."

"You won't need to mind—"

"Not all that much trouble," Ramsey said, pulling the team to a halt in the shade of a spreading cottonwood tree. "Tell me what you want taken inside."

Zoe turned to the Upchurches. "We won't need much, will we? Just a few clothes."

"That's all," Gideon said, struggling to rise. "Aim to get out and find a house to live in during the next few days. You best go tell Zeke and Sylvie what we're doing, Zoe."

"I'll see to it," Boone said, climbing down from the wagon seat.

The Parrishes had guessed or already knew what the plan was, as they were collecting items they would need for a brief stay in the hotel and placing them on the ground beside their vehicle.

"Sure nice here," Zeke said, glancing about. "Warm maybe, but real nice." He reached down, took up the two suitcases he had unloaded. Immediately he set one down.

"Was about to go without thanking you, Ramsey. Not sure we'd even be here if you hadn't come along when you did."

"I'm sure of it," Sylvie chimed in.

Boone took the man's hand, and then the woman's. "Glad to help."

"Will we see you again?" the woman asked.

"More'n likely."

"Fine—and good luck with the problem your brother's having at your ranch," Parrish said, picking up the suitcase again and starting for the hotel's door. "I'll come back and stable my horses if you don't mind seeing to Gideon's."

Boone turned to the Upchurch rig. Zoe and her aunt, not waiting for him, had succeeded in getting Gideon out of the wagon along with the necessary items they wished to take with them into the hostelry.

"Good luck, Ramsey," Upchurch said as, supported by his wife, he started for the side entrance to the hotel. "Sure can't thank you enough for all you've done."

"Forget it—"

"Want to beg your pardon, too, if my wife and me got a mite too personal talking to you."

"Can forget that, too," Boone said and nodded to Zoe. "I'll take those bags in for you."

The woman shook her head. "I can manage—you go on. I think you should get out to your ranch as soon as possible." She paused. "You said we'd meet again. When will that be?"

"Could be tonight—could be tomorrow. It's hard to say." He hesitated. "Just be waiting for me, is that enough of a promise?"

"It's enough," Zoe said and, stepping up to him, she kissed him squarely on the lips.

At once she turned away, took up the two bags, and headed for the hotel. Ramsey watched her slender figure with its shining red hair disappear into the building and then, moving to the front of the rig, he led the weary horses and the wagon to the stable in the rear.

Giving the hostler instructions and telling him Parrish would be along shortly with the second wagon, he released the sorrel and the buckskin from the rear of the Upchurch rig and, circling back to the street, pointed for the Border Saloon immediately south of it. Tying the two horses to the hitching rack, he went inside for the drink he'd promised himself.

Only a half dozen or so patrons were present, all cowhands from their dress, and none of them looked at all familiar. The bartender, however, was an old acquaintance.

"Boone Ramsey!" he shouted, extending his hand across the bar. "Been a passel of years since I've seen you."

"For a fact," Ramsey replied, searching his mind for the name of the bartender—a big, round-faced, hearty man with a howdy kind of a smile. Balding, dark-eyed, he was wearing a clean white apron over his street clothing.

"Sure am glad to see you back! Been hearing a lot of worrisome things about your ranch . . . What'll you have?"

"Whiskey with a beer on the side. What have you heard?" Ramsey replied, glancing about at the saloon's other customers, who had fallen silent at the bartender's jovial greeting.

"Been said that some other outfit's took it over and running it," the bartender said and, leaning forward, added in a low voice: "Real tough hard cases, I'm told."

"My brother, Curt—what about him?"

"He got hurt, you know," the bartender said, placing a shot glass of liquor and a mug of beer on the counter before Boone. "And they got him and Jubilee living in your folk's old house—just kicked them out of the regular ranch house. You know about that?"

Ramsey tossed off the whiskey, eased the burn with the beer. "No, sure hadn't," he said, laying a half dollar on the counter in payment for the drinks, "but I reckon I'll be finding out all about it real soon. I'm on my way to the ranch now."

The bartender, smiling, pushed the coin back to Boone. "This here's on the house. Don't want it ever said that Harry Parker don't appreciate his old customers . . . You say you're headed for the ranch?"

Boone nodded and picked up the half dollar. "Right away."

"Well, take care," Parker said, "and I'll be obliged if you don't repeat what I told you."

"Can bank on it," Ramsey said.

Wheeling, he crossed the quiet room to the swinging doors and stepped out into the warm daylight. Freeing his horses from the crossbar, he swung up onto the sorrel and, with the buckskin following closely, took the road that led southwest to Mesilla, and then on to Crosshatch.

16

Zoe paused just inside the hotel's side entrance and looked back, a sort of loneliness filling her. Boone had moved around to the front of the Upchurch wagon and, taking the bridle of the near leader horse in his hand, was starting for the livery barn some yards behind the hostelry.

She felt a tightness in her throat. Boone Ramsey fascinated her, had ever since the moment when she had seen him come riding headlong down that hill like some avenging angel to help them fight off the Indians. He had looked so fierce, so sure of himself, and when it was over and the savages had been driven off, it just seemed natural for him to take charge.

No man had ever affected her as did

Boone Ramsey and, thinking of that, she pictured him in her mind once again although he had been out of sight for only moments. She recalled how tall and wide-shouldered he was, how sun-browned, like saddle leather, his skin had become, thanks to years on the trail as he followed his profession. He had an easy, confident grace about him, like the panthers that roamed the Missouri Ozark hills, and he was at once all strength and will, despite the tenderness and compassion she had seen in him at times.

He had seemed surprised when she kissed him. Surely he had recognized how she felt about him. Boone was a man who had seen much of life and such would not have escaped him, just as she saw indications that he had more than a casual interest in her.

Zoe hoped that this was the way of it, that like all strong men Boone was loathe to reveal his feelings until he was sure of his ground. Would she ever see him again? That question crowded into her mind. Boone was a man accustomed to being on the move, of having no strings of any kind attached to him. He could shy away from any possibility of changing that, although Zoe knew for certain that she would be perfectly willing to accept the sort of life he had to offer her—even becoming a partner on the trail with him in his pursuit and capture of outlaws.

Outlaws . . . He was on his way to face several of them, all enemies of his brother Curt. Boone hadn't been too pleased with the prospect—not that he feared the outlaws, it was that he cared little about going to the aid of his brother. And thinking back over it, there had been a good chance he would have passed up Curt's trouble if Uncle Gideon hadn't lectured him at length on the duty of family members to stand by each other.

Uncle Gideon had been thinking of the Ozark country and the way families were there. Zoe wished now that he had kept quiet. Boone had said he would come back when the trouble had been settled, but she couldn't help thinking that something could go wrong, that the odds might prove too great for him and he'd—

"I'll take your suitcases, miss—"

Zoe came about at the unexpected words. The desk clerk, a man of about her age, wearing a stiff collar, polka dot bow tie along with a starched white shirt and blue suit, doubtless captivated by the sight of her standing there silhouetted in the doorway, had abandoned his post behind the desk and come forward to assist her.

"Your folks are on down the hall in Number Five," he said. "I'll be glad to take you and your bags to them."

Zoe smiled. "You're very kind," she murmured, and turned. At that moment she saw Boone Ramsey pass the front of the hotel on his way to get the drink he'd mentioned. The clerk, with the suitcases was moving off into the dark corridor leading from the lobby. Zoe followed slowly, a need to see Boone once more, maybe for the last time, pressing her mind. She trailed the clerk to room Number Five, entered when he politely knocked on the door and opened it, and allowed her to pass by.

"We've sent for a doctor," her aunt said as the clerk relinquished the bags. "Gideon's all right, but I thought it best we have the wound looked at."

"I'm glad you did," Zoe said. "Do you need me for anything?"

Sadie Upchurch considered her niece thoughtfully. "Is it Boone Ramsey?"

Zoe nodded. "I just want to see him once more—tell him good-bye again."

"I thought he said he'd come back—"

"I know, but I'm not sure—and I'm a little afraid. He's gone to have it out with those outlaws, and—"

"You run along," Sadie said kindly. "I'm sure he'll be all right—and thank him again for us."

Zoe returned to the hallway, hurriedly crossed the lobby to the front doorway, and stepped out onto the board sidewalk that extended across the building's width. Boone had said something about the saloon being close by. She glanced around. The Border Queen was right next door. In that same instant her spirits fell. Boone had been in the saloon, had his drink, and was now riding off down the street.

Impulsively Zoe took a dozen hasty steps after him. She paused, started to call out to him, but thought better of it. Troubled by thoughts of what lay ahead for him at the ranch, it was best he not be distracted. Anyway, she'd made it clear how she felt about him—it was up to him to make the next move now insofar as their relationship was concerned.

"That's Boone Ramsey—sure'n hell—"

At the words Zoe turned. Three hard-looking men had come out of the Border

Queen, were standing on the walk staring after Boone.

"Ain't seen him in a few years, but you sure don't forget a jasper like him. Anyway, you heard what Parker called him."

"It's Ramsey, all right—but he ain't so much that a bullet won't stop him," the shorter of the three said dryly.

The man who had spoken first, a thick-shouldered individual wearing a red-and-black-checked shirt along with other ordinary cowhand clothing, agreed. "That's for damn sure, but we best get out to the ranch and let Phin know this hell-for-leather brother of Curt's is in town."

"That's where he's headed—ain't no doubt of that," the third of the party, an ordinary-looking man wearing a high crowned hat, said. "Phin'll want to be ready for him."

"Ain't sure he'll be there," checked shirt said. "He was aiming to go to Cruces."

"Well, then, I reckon that leaves it up to us to take care of Mister Boone Ramsey," the short, squat puncher said.

"About right. We can circle around, cut across country, and be waiting for him in them rocks this side of that big draw."

The two outlaws nodded their assent to

their companion's suggestion. One reached up, gave his hat a tug, pulling it down on his head more firmly.

"Let's get hopping. He'd done got a pretty good start on us, and we sure want to be all set when we go up against him. The way I've heard it, he ain't an easy man to kill."

Cold chills raced through Zoe Tillman. This apparently was what Boone was up against continually. These three men were evidently part of the outlaw gang that had taken over the Ramsey ranch. One thing was clear: they were planning to kill Boone as he rode to help his brother. Taut, she watched the outlaws cross to their horses, mount, and head back up the street.

At once she turned. She just couldn't stand there—she had to warn Boone. Hurrying into the hotel, she went up to the clerk now behind his desk.

"Will you tell my folks that I had to leave—go for a ride, you can say. Tell them not to worry," she said and, before he could make an answer, moved on.

Leaving the hotel by the side door, Zoe ran the short distance to the stable. Breathless, she faced the hostler, busy at removing the harness from the Parrish team.

"I need a horse and saddle. Have you got one I can use?"

"Rent—that what you mean?" The hostler, an old man with a white beard and wearing bib overalls, paused at his work to consider the woman. "Reckon I have . . . Ain't you one of them folks that just drove in?"

"Yes—yes, I am. Please, have you got a horse I can use? I have to catch up with Boone—the man who was driving our wagon. There's three men, they're going to kill him if—"

"Take that little mare in the last stall," the hostler said, concern filling his eyes. "She's all saddled and ready to ride. You sure I can't do—"

"Thank you," Zoe said, hurrying away. "He just needs to be warned, and I can do that."

Running to the Upchurch wagon, she brushed aside the old lap robe that covered the rifle left on the seat. Taking it up, she checked the magazine, found it full and then, circling the vehicle, ran to the last stall, where the hostler had said a horse was waiting.

The mare, a well-fed gray, saddled and bridled as the stableman noted, shied nervously as Zoe entered the stall. Paying no mind, the woman freed the lines and backed the horse into the runway. Putting a foot in the stirrup and grasping the horn, Zoe pulled herself up into the saddle. Quickly cutting the mare about, she rode up to the hostler and paused.

"How do I get to the Ramsey place—the Crosshatch Ranch?"

"Just take the road out of town to Mesilla, then when you come to a fork, keep to the right-hand road. It'll take you to the Ramsey place."

Zoe nodded and, drumming the sides of the mare with her heels, left the stable at a fast run.

17

All the way to the stagecoach station Jesse Ramsey had maintained a close watch on the country around him and Hannah Bradley for the three outlaws. He was certain they had not seen the last of them. For one thing, he and Hannah had been witnesses to the murder of the Shotgun, and possibly of driver Tom Donovan if the older man failed to make it, when the coach was ambushed, and the outlaws could not afford to let them live, and talk.

Too, pride would play a big part in the way they looked at the situation. One man had bested them—a party of five—had actually killed two of them and taken from them a woman whom they had intended to have great sport with. That, possibly, to the three remaining renegades would be the most dominant force demanding revenge.

But although Jesse kept a sharp watch on the flats, the slopes, and the deep arroyos, the outlaws had not put in an appearance by the time he and Hannah rode into Jimson Station. There a man, apparently the agent worried by the failure of the coach to arrive, hurried out to meet them.

"You from the westbound stage? There something wrong?" he shouted in a rush of words. A tall, spare individual with angular features and iron-gray hair, his concern for the stage and its passengers was like a dark mantle hanging over him.

Jesse nodded and swung off his horse. Donovan had not made it to the way station as yet. Evidently he was hurt worse than it was thought, Ramsey guessed as he helped Hannah dismount. Three other men and a woman had now come out of the station and were close by listening.

"My name's Willoby. I'm the agent here," the tall man said. "What happened?"

"Holdup, about ten miles east of here. Five men. The shotgun was killed and your driver, Tom Donovan, hurt. He was going to come on in—I figured he'd be here before now," Ramsey said and finished, giving a full account of the incident.

Willoby turned to the other men. "Joe, you and Clint and Morley mount up and go get Donovan and the coach."

"Poor Kelly," the woman murmured. "He was hoping to get a job driving real soon. Too bad."

"Sure is," the station agent said. "How'd you and the lady—"

"Outlaws rode off with her. Soon as I could, I followed and caught up with them. You'll find one of your horses and two of the outlaws a mile or so east of where the coach is."

"You have to shoot it out with them?"

Jesse glanced to where the woman, likely the agent's wife, arm around Hannah, was moving slowly toward the building. He nodded, dismissing any further explanation, and then said: "Tell your men to stay on the road. Donovan'll be somewhere along it."

Taking the reins of the two outlaw horses he had appropriated for his and Hannah's use, Ramsey started for the stable behind the way station.

"Like to feed and rest my animals for the night. Expect to head out early in the morning."

Willoby looked at him in surprise. "The stage'll be ready to leave about seven—"

"I figure it's best I go on horseback. Can cut across country, save time."

"What about the lady? She be going along with you?" the agent wondered, moving up beside Jesse as he headed for the barn.

"Best you ask her," Ramsey said.

They reached the stable and, with Willoby assisting, stripped the horses, poured a measure of grain into the feed box of the manger, and threw down a forkful of hay.

"I'll see they get watered," Willoby said as they started back to the main building. "Expect you and the lady'll be needing different rooms?"

"You figure right," Jesse said, and made no further explanation.

Inside they found Hannah sitting at the end of the long dining table drinking coffee.

Jesse sat down beside her and poured himself a cup of the dark hot brew from the tin pot.

"Like to know if you'll be taking the morning stage," Willoby said. "It'll be leaving about seven o'clock."

Hannah, her lovely features set now to worn, weary lines, glanced at Jesse. "What are you doing?"

"I'm staying in the saddle. It'll save time," he replied.

"Then I'm going with you," Hannah said promptly.

Ramsey shook his head. "Be a hard trip. Not sure you could stand it. I figure it'll be better for you to go on in the coach."

"I don't—and there's no need to worry about riding horseback being too hard on me. My back aches a little now, but I'll get over that. What time do you want to leave?"

"First light, but I'm not sure—"

"I'll be ready," Hannah said decisively, putting an end to the discussion. "Will we need food for the trail? If so I can—"

"Not much—just a little lunch. We ought to reach Mesilla by the middle of the afternoon, providing we don't run into trouble."

Hannah paused, cup halfway to her

mouth. "You're thinking about those out-laws—"

Ramsey said, "Yes, that's it. I'm not banking on them giving up." He started to add that she would likely be much safer in the stagecoach than with him, and then left it unsaid. His words would carry little assurance after what had already happened to her while a passenger in one of the big vehicles.

"I want you to be sure of what you're doing," he said after a time.

Hannah studied him thoughtfully. Out in the nearby stable some sort of commotion was taking place, one of the horses tangled in its harness most likely.

"Are you trying to tell me that you don't want me riding with you?"

"No, not that," Ramsey said. "Just that it'll be hard going. I aim to travel fast, try to make up for lost time. Could be I'll be getting to the ranch too late as it is."

Hannah gave him a quiet, confident smile. "I won't slow you down—and I'll be ready to go at first light," she said and, rising, followed the agent's wife to her room.

Willoby, sitting nearby, chuckled. "Son, there ain't no use arguing with a woman in love. Learned that myself a long time ago."

"In love—with me?" Ramsey echoed, frowning.

Willoby snorted. "You're mighty blind if you can't see that, mister," he said, getting to his feet. "I'll see you at supper—and you best let my woman doctor up your head."

Next morning Hannah was as good as her word. She came to the stable just as the sky in the east was brightening, bringing with her the bag that had been in the coach and had been brought in late that previous night, and a sack of lunch Mrs. Willoby had prepared.

Jesse, his duster recovered from the coach also, had readied the horses and, throwing out the miscellaneous items he found in the outlaw's saddlebags, replaced them with possessions of his own. He had gone over the bridles and saddles as well, even shortening the stirrups of the horse Hannah would be riding so that she would be more comfortable.

There was a rifle in the boot of the bay that he had taken and, finding only a few cartridges, Jesse purchased a half box from Willoby, who maintained a small stock of ammunition and other salable articles at one end of the way station. Shedding his coat, as he knew they would be going into much warmer country, Jesse drew on his duster and then, helping Hannah up onto her horse, mounted the bay.

"Feels much better since you fixed the stirrups," she said, settling herself. "Thank you."

"We've got a long way to go. Wanted you to be as comfortable as possible," Ramsey said, and turned his attention to the Willobys standing nearby. "Donovan was sleeping when I dropped by to see him. Be obliged if you'll tell him I said *adios*, and that I hope he'll be on his feet soon."

"Be glad to," the station agent said.

Jesse nodded, touched the brim of his hat with a forefinger, and glanced at Hannah. "I reckon we're ready to move out."

"Yes, I reckon we are," Hannah said with a smile.

Jesse swung his horse about and, leaving the yard with Hannah at his side, headed off across the flat on which the way station had been built, in a southwesterly fashion.

"Good luck!" he heard Willoby call as they rode past the station building.

Ramsey lifted his hand in reply. They would need it if the three outlaws were still somewhere in the area searching for them, he thought.

"Have you always lived in this part of the country?" Hannah asked an hour or so later as, abreast, they rode steadily on.

Jesse had put the horses to an easy lope, one calculated to cover distance without unduly tiring them

"Was born back east—in Pennsylvania," he said. "My folks moved out here when I was about six. Lived on the ranch near Mesilla until I moved out a few years ago."

Hannah brushed at her face with a small handkerchief and sighed. "I've never been able to get used to the emptiness of this country. There's so much open land with nothing in sight but plains, and maybe a hill now and then."

"Plenty of high mountains on to the north—the Sandias and the Sangre de Cristos, to mention a couple of ranges. And down here near Mesilla and Las Cruces we've got the Organs."

"But things are so dry! Where I came from there were rivers—real rivers—and streams, and the land was covered by grass and there were lots of trees."

"You'll find it like that along the Rio Grande, the river that runs by Cruces and Mesilla. Some of the cottonwoods growing beside it are six foot through the trunk and are maybe fifty foot tall."

Hannah unbuttoned the light cotton jacket she had pulled on at the way station. She had replaced the torn shirtwaist with one of darker color.

"I'll be happy to see something like that," she said, and lapsed into silence.

They rode on continually, bearing in a southwesterly direction for several hours, with only an occasional word passing between them. Late in the morning they halted in the filigree shade of a large mesquite to rest the horses as well as themselves. Uncorking his canteen, he offered it to Hannah, who took a sip of the tepid water, and then had a swallow himself.

"I was thinking about the driver of the stagecoach," Hannah said, sitting down on a small, sandy hummock. "Do you think he'll be all right? When he wasn't at the way station I thought he had died—and all because of me."

Jesse, in the act of moistening the horses' mouths and lips with a wet rag, looked at her in surprise. "Why would you say that—that it would have been your fault?"

"If you could have stayed with him instead of going after me—and those outlaws, you—"

"Doubt if it would have made any difference. Willoby figures Donovan will make it, anyway. They found him about halfway along the road to the station. He'd fallen off his horse. I guess he'd lost a lot of blood, but—"

Ramsey paused, came to attention. Three riders had just topped out a rise a quarter mile or so to the east. He turned quickly, hung the canteen back on his saddle.

"We've got company," he said quietly.

18

Hannah came to her feet at once and put her attention on the distant riders. "Do you think they're those outlaws—the ones that—"

"Can't be dead sure," Jesse said, freeing the horses' reins from the mesquite, "but I'd say yes. Mount up. We won't take any chance. Best we keep as much distance as we can between them and us."

Hannah didn't wait to be assisted but thrust a foot in the stirrup and, gathering her full skirt in her right hand, grasped the saddle horn and pulled herself up onto her horse. Jesse, close by on the bay, immediately led off. They were crossing a broad mesa broken occasionally by more clumps of mesquite, bayonet yucca, chaparral, and other similar dry country growth which would appear to support no forms of life, yet birds were plentiful and long-eared jackrabbits bolted out from the clumps of brush frequently. The only break in the sameness of the land appeared to be some miles on ahead, where the mesa seemed to break up into an area of bluffs and buttes.

"We've got to make it to there," Jesse said, pointing as he put the horses to a faster lope. "Can shake them off our trail then—if we're lucky."

It was difficult to talk at the now-hurried pace of the horses. Hannah said nothing until they reached the outcrop of the broken land and had ridden down into a narrow arroyo screened by Apache plume, rabbit brush, and scrub oak.

"Are they still following us?" she asked, a tightness about her mouth.

Jesse halted at a slight rise in the wash and, standing in his stirrups, looked back. The outlaws, riding hard with no thought as to the condition of their horses, it appeared, had gained considerable ground. That the outlaws had spotted them earlier was evident, after which it was easy for the renegades to keep them in sight as they crossed the near-flat mesa.

"They're still coming," he replied. Sparing her nothing, he added: "Not too far behind us now."

"What can we do?"

"Try to lose them, that's the only thing we can," Jesse said tersely and, urging the bay forward, led the way down into the arroyo.

A half mile or so on the wash deepened and forked. The cut of the left looked to be smaller, more heavily overgrown and littered with rocks. Immediately Ramsey turned into the right-hand division. He continued on for a short distance and then, climbing out, cut back across the sandy, gravel-and brush-covered ground to the other fork.

"We'll hole up here, let them think we took the other fork," he said as he drew to a stop behind a stand of mesquite.

Hannah watched him dismount and then followed suit. "You mean to just let them go on by?" she said. The heat had increased, and she now turned to removing her jacket.

"What I'm hoping they'll do," Jesse replied, brushing at the sweat laying on his forehead with the back of a hand. "I figure they will if they don't see our tracks where we turned off."

Hannah said nothing as he removed the duster he was wearing and stuffed it into a saddlebag pocket, after which he moved to face the point where the outlaws would be entering the arroyo.

"Why don't you just shoot them when they come in sight?" she asked, puzzled.

Jesse turned to her. Her face was chalk white as she was remembering what she went through at the hands of the outlaws, and her eyes were bright with anger.

"You're talking about murder," he said quietly.

"Maybe it is, but what's the difference? They'll kill us if they get the chance—and thinking of what they planned to do to me, why, I don't think they deserve any consideration. I can't understand you, Jesse—you killed two of them!"

"It's one thing to shoot down a man when you have to, something else to murder him—"

Hannah shook her head. "I can't see the difference. He's dead either way."

Ramsey smiled. Hannah was beautiful when she was angry; her cheeks glowed and her brown eyes sparkled. He recalled what Station Agent Willoby had said about her—about the futility of arguing with a woman in love. Willoby, of course, was unaware of the facts; but it would be wonderful if he were free to return her feelings.

"It's a bit hard to explain, but there is a difference. And it's a hell of a thing to kill a man—any man. You rob him of his life. I've never done it unless I had no choice, and then I regretted it."

"Well, I find it hard to see it your way," Hannah said, stepping up to Jesse's horse and drawing the rifle from its boot. "It wouldn't bother me to shoot any of the outlaw bunch."

"It won't bother me either if it comes down to a shootout," Jesse said, taking the weapon from her. "I'll give this back to you if it becomes necessary, otherwise just stay quiet and let them ride by."

Color still filled Hannah's cheeks, and angry tears now added to the brightness of her eyes. "If they try—"

"Don't worry about them bothering you again," Ramsey said. "They'll have to climb over me first—and I don't plan on them doing that." He raised up slightly and looked to the upper end of the arroyo. "Here they come."

The outlaws reached the fork in the arroyo. The one in the lead, a squat-looking, dark man, was studying the ground before him.

"I heard them call him Pike," Hannah whispered. "The one behind him is Jace Thompson. Last one is Chino."

The three men drew to a stop. Pike pulled off his battered hat and rubbed at the shine on his forehead. "They kept a'going," he said. "Can't see them, but they're ahead somewhere."

"Lot of brush. They could just be hiding," Thompson commented. "You figure catching up with them's worth all this here hard riding?"

Jesse cast a side glance at Hannah. She was rigid, frozen. He reached out and laid his hand on her arm. She smiled, appeared to relax slightly.

"Been wondering that, too," the one called Chino said. "Now, I ain't so sure I want to go up against that jasper the girl's with. He sure put Henry and Bart under without batting an eye!"

"Hell, I ain't afeard of him," Pike said.

"He was plain lucky back there—caught us not looking . . . Come on, let's keep moving."

The outlaws resumed the faint, ragged trail, taking for granted that the horse tracks along the right wing of the fork did not end but continued on down the wash. Jesse allowed a good half hour to pass and then walked to a high place in the arroyo and turned his attention into the direction the outlaws had taken. He nodded in satisfaction. The three men, now well to the south, were but blurred, dark figures in the distance. Pivoting, he returned to where Hannah and the horses waited.

"They're gone," he said, and watched relief spread across the woman's features. "You can forget about them."

Hannah smiled at him apologetically as they mounted. "I—I don't know what came over me, but I'm sure I would have shot and killed any one of those men if I'd had a gun."

"Expect you had good reason to feel that way," Ramsey said and, doubling back to the forks, cut completely away and struck a straight course for Mesilla.

An hour or so later they halted beneath a lone cottonwood tree growing in a sink and ate lunch while the horses rested, and Jesse again swabbed their mouths with a wet rag. The delay was short and they were soon again in the saddle, riding now with a slanting sun shining on their faces.

"Haven't had a chance to tell you, but you're a lot better on a horse than I expected," Ramsey said as they pressed on. "Any woman I ever knew could not stand staying in the saddle like you have."

"I'm used to riding," Hannah said. "Up in Wichita there was a rancher I became acquainted with. He'd come by about every day and we'd go for long rides along the Arkansas River. I got quite used to a saddle."

"I reckon that explains it," Jesse said. "When we get to Mesilla you get yourself a room at the inn—I'll see to stabling your horse. I think you'd best stay out of sight for the rest of the day and evening. Don't think Pike and the others will double back this way, but it's hard to figure what they might do."

Hannah nodded. After a few moments she said, "Will I see you again before I go on to El Paso?" It was a tentatively placed question, filled with hope.

Ramsey was quiet for a time while he

considered her words. Finally he shrugged. "Hard to make any plans until I know how things are with my brother."

"You're going to help him?"

Jesse nodded. Smoke in the distance marked the location of Las Cruces, while a smaller gray smudge in the sky beyond indicated Mesilla.

"Finally got it sorted out in my mind. Seems I've got no choice."

"I see—and I guess I understand," Hannah said with a deep sigh. "I'll worry about you."

"No need—"

"What about me—and El Paso?" she asked boldly. "Will you be going on with me when you're finished helping your brother?"

The words spoken by Willoby at the Jimson way station again came to Ramsey's mind. He needed to be careful—and kind. If he didn't have other commitments back in Redrock—

"Haven't looked that far ahead."

"I see," the woman murmured. "Let's leave it this way—I'll wait two days at the inn. If I haven't seen or heard from you after that, I'll know you're not coming."

"Or that I'm dead," Ramsey said jokingly.

"I'll never believe that. I think you'd be a hard man to kill, Jesse Ramsey—so I'll be waiting for you."

Waiting for you. Jesse gave that deeper consideration. He hadn't thought much about Ruby Bellman since leaving Redrock. She was waiting, too—along with the saloon and gambling casino he had worked so hard to build up. A wry smile pulled at his lips. He would have to make a choice—being with Hannah had somehow changed the way he looked at things—and it was a decision he'd have to make when the trouble at Crosshatch was settled.

19

Boone Ramsey, riding reluctantly across the land on his way to Crosshatch, let his gaze drift over the range. It looked good—*prime fodder*, his father would have termed it. Evidently the country had enjoyed a wet spring, which was further attested to by the strong flow of the river and the thickly leafed limbs of the big cottonwood trees, which appeared to reach out farther than usual. Even the brush was lush and green, and birds—meadowlarks, doves, jays, quail, thrashers, and mimicking mockingbirds—were everywhere.

But there were no cattle to be seen. Curt had bragged that one day he would have Crosshatch range covered with cattle, eight or maybe ten thousand head. It was a dream, Boone knew. Still there should be a few hundred, or maybe a thousand, in sight. Could the lack have something to do with the outlaw problem that Jubilee had mentioned? Or could it be simply that the stock was off grazing on some distant part of the ranch?

Maybe Curt had lost the entire herd to the outlaws; perhaps that was what the trouble was all about—and if so, then it was Curt's lookout, not his. The bartender in the Border Queen had said that Curt and Jubilee were now living in the old ranch house to where, as the bartender had indicated, they had been driven by the outlaws. From the sound of that the renegades, whoever they were, had actually taken over Crosshatch—which was again, to his way of thinking, something Curt had to deal with.

Boone scrubbed irritably at the stubble on his chin. Goddam Curt anyway! There

Pa had worked and starved to build Cross-hatch into a fine, prosperous cattle ranch —and so had he along with Curt and Jesse, and Jubilee, not to mention what their mother had endured to make the place a success.

Boone swore. He reckoned he was in between a rock and a hard place. Maybe he didn't give a hoot for Curt and his wife, but he'd be damned if he'd stand by and let a bunch of no-account, stinking outlaws have the place and thereby reap the benefits of the family's hard work.

He glanced ahead. A rough, ragged break in the usually smooth land lay before him. Wild, brushy, and littered with rocks, it was a tangled brake that was a continual curse to the ranch. He recalled how old Eben had termed it a hellhole and despised every foot of it, and wished often for a way to rid himself of the troublesome area of his ranch. Cattle strayed into it, some by accident, others, usually mean, ornery old longhorns that deserted the herds; coyotes, wolves, rattlesnakes, even cougars made it their favored haunt.

Boone had always hated the annual springtime chore of riding into it and hazing out—brush popping—the stock that was hiding in the dense brush and rocks.

Ramsey slowed as he reached the gravelly, uneven surface of the trail leading down into the swalelike area. A hawk, startled by his approach, sailed gracefully off to one side, sharp, yellow eyes fixed on horse and rider. In the afternoon sunlight the redtail took on a sleek appearance, as if it had just bathed its feathers in oil of some kind.

The sorrel, followed closely by the buckskin, moved slowly, taking care with each step as he descended the path. Boone let him have his way, aware that the big, trailwise gelding knew exactly what he was doing. One misplaced iron-shod hoof on the weather-worn, rounded rocks in the trail could cause him to fall, and he was instinctively doing his utmost to avoid such an accident.

They reached the bottom of the slope and broke out onto the sandy floor of an arroyo. Boone drew to a halt, intending to let the sweaty sorrel breathe and settle down. Suddenly a hunched figure rose out of the brush off to the right. Instantly and without conscious thought, Ramsey rocked to one side and drew his gun.

He triggered his weapon in the same instant as the man hiding in the brush. Boone felt a bullet rip through the slack in his sleeve as he came out of the saddle and dropped to a crouch on the sandy ground. Whether his hastily fired bullet had found its target he had no way of telling. Only one thing was certain: the bushwhacker was no longer to be seen.

Keeping low, Ramsey moved quickly to the side and took shelter behind a large boulder. Not stopping there, weapon ready in his hand, he worked his way around the misshapen mass of sandstone, narrowed eyes whipping back and forth as he searched for the man who had attempted to ambush him.

Who the hell was it? One of the outlaws who had driven Curt out of the family house and forcibly taken over Crosshatch? If true, how did they know he was a Ramsey? Or was it an old enemy, a family member of some outlaw he'd brought in to face justice who was now seeking vengeance. There were many of them, he knew—all that he'd accumulated over the years and expected he'd be forced to reckon with before he drew a last breath.

He could see no one. Insects were buzzing in the brush and a rattlesnake lay coiled in the shade of another large rock a short distance away, unaware of his presence. Hunched against the hot surface of a boulder, Boone waited patiently. How often had he been through a similar situation, moments when he had lain low, watching for some wanted criminal to appear so that he could take the man in hand; or the times when he himself, trapped by several outlaws and backed into a corner, had hung motionless in a vacuum of silence while he sought a way out.

Brush whispered softly just beyond a weedy pile of sand and rocks to his left. The sound came from nowhere near where the bushwhacker had been hiding. Either the man had moved completely away or there were more than one in the party.

Keeping low, Ramsey continued to work his way around the boulder, through a stand of Apache plume to another large rock. There he halted again and, with sweat shining on his sun darkened face and dampening his body, once more listened.

Somewhere a quail was calling forlornly into the afternoon's hush. The rattlesnake had not moved, and several cicadas were setting up a racket in a small stand of cottonwoods back up the slope.

Ramsey could see or hear nothing, and

after a long ten minutes he raised himself cautiously to his full height for a complete look around. The sorrel, he saw, had drifted off the trail a short distance, and was tugging and chewing at a clump of bunch grass. Nearby the buckskin had also found forage for himself.

Boone came slowly about. He'd be better off at the big rock near the sorrel, where the bushwhacker had first taken a shot at him. Bent low, on hands and knees at times, Ramsey retraced his steps to his original position.

At his first move insects in the close-by brush ceased, but the rattler remained indifferent. It had taken several minutes as he had moved slowly and quietly, but he'd made it without drawing the bushwhacker's —if there were only one—fire.

Mopping at the sweat on his face again, he drew himself erect at the side of the oversize boulder and, leaning against its scorching surface, again made a survey of the surrounding area.

Abruptly he pivoted and put his attention on the trail leading down into the arroyo. The definite click of a horse's iron shoe striking rock had reached his straining ears. The bushwhacker, or bushwhackers, whoever they happened to be, were endeavoring to box him in.

A hard grin pulled at Boone Ramsey's mouth, and his flat-planed cornered features settled into an expression of grimness. Sinking lower beside the boulder, he leveled his six-gun on the point in the trail where the oncoming rider would first appear.

Eyes squeezed down to lessen the glare, Boone kept his gaze fixed on the trail. The click of metal on stone came again. Ramsey tensed. The bobbing head of a gray horse came into view. Thumbing back the hammer of his gun—masking the sound by cupping his hand over the weapon—Ramsey waited.

20

It was Zoe Tillman.

Relaxing, Boone swore softly. Zoe, hunched forward on the horse she was riding, was staring ahead. Her hair was a bright gold in the sunlight—the color of aspen leaves in the fall, he thought—and her features were taut and strained, having lost their usual softness and taken on a paleness.

Lowering his weapon, Ramsey pulled

away from the boulder. "Here," he said in a low voice and, stepping hurriedly to her side, he halted the gray and all but dragged her from the saddle.

"What the hell are you doing here?" he demanded, pulling her into the shelter of the rock. "You want to get yourself killed?"

Zoe, breathless from his quick, decisive action, managed a deep sigh. "Thank God, you're all right. I heard those gunshots—"

"One was mine, the other came from some jasper trying to bushwhack me. He missed. Now, I want to know why you're here."

"I came looking for you. Wanted to catch up and warn you that three men—they looked like regular cowhands—were planning to get out ahead of you, and shoot you as you rode to your ranch," Zoe explained, and related what she had overheard the men say as they stood in front of the saloon. She had immediately gotten herself a horse from the stable and set out to warn him.

"I—I thought when I heard the shooting that I was too late. Oh, Boone—I'm so thankful that you're alive!"

Boone grinned. "I'm a mite hard to kill —been quite a few that found that out. You say there were three of them?"

Zoe nodded. "One of them had recognized you. And they mentioned somebody named Phin—said that he ought to be warned so's he could be ready for you, but they weren't sure he was at the ranch."

"Phin . . . I expect that's the name of the head honcho that Curt's having trouble with. Anything else?"

"Only that they planned to circle around and head you off at some rocks."

"Just what they've done," Boone said, "only the first shot one of them got at me missed." He opened the loading gate of his .45 and, rodding out the spent cartridge, replaced it with a fresh one.

"You oughtn't be here, Zoe," he said. "Could get yourself hurt—maybe killed."

She smiled. "Maybe I don't kill easy either. I brought my rifle so I could help."

"Best thing you could do is turn around and head back to town—but I'm scared that wouldn't be safe with Phin's bunch hanging around here somewhere."

Zoe nodded, pleased. "You're right. Smart thing for me to do is stay right here with you."

Ramsey eyed her critically. She was the best-looking woman he'd ever laid eyes on, and she had spunk to go with it.

184

"All right, but you'll do what I say, and that's stay right here by this rock. Savvy?"

"Savvy?" She frowned, unfamiliar with the word so common along the frontier.

"I'm saying—do you understand?"

Zoe smiled. "If that's what you want me to do, I'll do it—but I want my rifle."

Boone made no reply and, keeping low, crossed to where her gray had joined the sorrel and the buckskin packhorse at grazing on the small island of grass. Pulling the rifle from the boot of the gray's saddle, he returned to where the woman waited.

"I don't want you using this unless you have to—"

Zoe frowned. "Then what's the point of me—"

"Best they don't know where you are. If you shoot it'll draw their fire."

Zoe's shoulders stirred resignedly. "All right, if that's what you want. What are you going to do?"

"Roust them out," Ramsey said and started to turn away. He paused, leaned over, and kissed her on the lips. "That's for luck. I've got a hunch you bring it to me," he added and moved silently off into the dense brush.

After what Zoe had told him the outlaws

had said, Ramsey was certain they had not given up but were still around, probably ducking in and out of the rocks and brush looking for a chance to put a bullet into him. The answer to that was to find them first; he'd learned long ago that it was better to take the initiative at such times, change from being the hunted to the hunter. The advantage would be with him then, and that to Boone's way of thinking was all important when death was to be the final outcome.

Crouched low, gun ready, he moved slowly and quietly on. The rattlesnake had vanished, he noted, as he drew near the boulder where he'd seen the serpent. Likely it had sought out a cooler place as the sun now beat directly down on the spot where it had lain coiled.

Where the hell were the outlaws? He was in no mood to be playing hide-and-seek. Seems he should at least glimpse one of them. He hesitated, looked up the slope. Could they have placed themselves above him, finding for themselves hiding places along the foot of the low bluff that over-looked the arroyo? With rifles they could command not only the trail below but the slope as well.

That had to be the answer, Boone decided, and continuing on until he came to a tall stand of brush, he changed directions and started making his way toward the red-faced escarpment. A cottontail burst suddenly from the weeds and rocks in front of him and raced off toward the floor of the wash. Boone cursed. If the outlaws were maintaining a sharp watch, they would guess that something had frightened the rabbit and that it likely was him. At once he veered from the the direction he was taking and began to follow a course several strides to its left.

"You hear that, Pete?"

The guarded voice was startlingly close. Ramsey froze, then turned to the direction it had come from. It was to his left and slightly above.

"Was a damned rabbit. Seen it go running down toward the wash."

"Well, something scared it up—"

"Maybe. Could've been a snake, or maybe a coyote. Cottontails are mighty jumpy."

Boone, again moving cautiously, crouched low. Taking each step with care, he approached the apparent location of the nearest man. The second outlaw, Pete, was higher up.

Abruptly a man was standing in the brush directly before Ramsey. He stared at Boone in amazement, and then his mouth flew open.

"By God, here he is!" he yelled in a hoarse voice.

Ramsey drove a bullet into the outlaw's chest before he could fire the weapon he leveled. As the man staggered back and fell, Boone rushed forward. Pete, a few yards up the slope, was on his feet, gun blasting. Ramsey, dodging from side to side, continued his headlong charge up the slope. Shortly, heaving for breath, leg muscles screaming in pain at the effort put to them, he halted.

Pete, a squat bearded man in old, faded army clothing and wearing a northern campaign hat, stepped from behind a large rock and, gun leveled, faced Boone. The grin on his lips faded as Ramsey's bullet, fired a fraction of time before he could get off his shot, smashed into his body and sent him tumbling down the slope.

Boone, tall frame taut, muscles keyed to instant action, replaced the spent cartridges in his weapon as the recurring echoes faded gradually and powder smoke mingling with dust drifted across the slope. Gun ready, he waited for some indication of the third outlaw's whereabouts. The answer came almost immediately.

"You all get him?" a voice, somewhat below where Ramsey expected it to be, called out. "What happened up there?"

Ramsey wheeled quickly and began to descend the grade. Within only a half dozen steps he located the outlaw crouched beside a clump of oak brush.

"Dead—that's how they are," Boone said quietly. "Drop that gun or you'll be keeping them company."

The outlaw, young, ordinary-looking, and wearing a high crowned hat and large Mexican spurs with long tines, got to his feet slowly as he relinquished his weapon.

"Now, back away from it—and keep your hands up where I can see them. You try something and—"

"I ain't figuring to try nothing, mister," the outlaw said hurriedly. "No sir, I purely ain't."

Boone moved forward and picked up the gun. Thrusting it under his belt, he said: "Where's your horse?"

"Right over yonder," the outlaw said, jerking a thumb in the direction of a stand of mesquite.

"I want you to load up your partners on their horses, then you're going to mount up and move out with them."

The younger man frowned. "Where'll I take them?"

"That's up to you—they're your friends," Ramsey said, and motioned with his gun. "Get at it."

Walking behind the thin-faced outlaw, Boone followed him to where the dead men lay. Moving around the younger man each time, Ramsey kicked their weapons off into the brush and stepped back.

"Drag them down to the horses—"

"Drag them?"

"Drag them or carry them—makes no difference to me," Ramsey said.

The outlaw shrugged and, first taking the man called Pete by the heels, moved him to the small clearing behind the mesquite, after which he returned for the second outlaw. That done, and struggling a bit with the chore as Boone made no effort to assist him, he loaded the bodies across their saddles, tied them down, and then swung up onto his own horse.

"Expect you're going to have to reach me them reins," he said.

Ramsey, gun trained on the youthful outlaw, gathered up the leathers of the two other horses and handed them to him.

"Sure don't know which way to go. And toting Pete and Dave, being dead, I sure ain't—"

"Head any direction but west," Boone said. "The border's south, and it ain't far. Maybe that's where you best go—and if you try doubling back I'll kill you."

The outlaw nodded. "Yes, sir, I savvy. But what am I going to do with Pete and Dave?"

"Could take them by the graveyard in town and dump them off," Boone said. "Maybe somebody'll come along and bury them."

"Yeah, maybe so," the outlaw said and, swinging about, he headed south along the slope.

Ramsey watched the slim young man for a full five minutes until he and the two horses he was leading were well into the distance, and then cut back to where Zoe was waiting.

"It's me," he called out well ahead of time. "Don't shoot."

Zoe was on her feet. Relief filled her eyes and her slender body was rigid with tension.

"That shooting—I was about to start looking for you," she said. "I was afraid that—"

"You best set your mind to never worrying about me and gunshots," Ramsey said, taking her by the arm and moving toward the horses. "Otherwise you'll be spending a lot of time stewing around."

Zoe smiled down at him as she settled into her saddle. "I'm beginning to think I'll have no reason to worry about anything as long as I'm with you."

Ramsey, one foot in the stirrup, hesitated before going on up onto his horse. "That something you just decided?"

Zoe brushed at the moisture on her forehead and cheeks with a handkerchief. "No, I think I made up my mind to that back there when those Indians attacked us, and you came riding down that hill to help."

"I see," Boone said, and for a long breath was silent. Far off to the north a flock of ducks were winging their way up the river, and he seemed lost in the contemplation of them. Finally he stirred.

"That's something we'll have to talk about," he said, and finished mounting the sorrel. "Right now I want you to turn that horse around and head back to town. Won't be safe around here for you."

Zoe shook her head. "What I want is to be with you," she said in a firm voice.

Boone studied the firm, stubborn set of her lips. He smiled faintly. "All right, have it your way. Let's go see what kind of a fix my brother's gone and got himself into."

21

The outlaw who, with a dozen of his kind, had driven Curt and Jubilee out of the ranch house and taken over Crosshatch was Phin Durbin, Barnaby, the hostler at the livery barn in Mesilla, had told Jesse when he asked. A real hard case, shoot-out bunch, the stableman had described them. It was no big wonder that Curt and Jubilee found themselves in the hole they were in.

"Hole?" Jesse had repeated.

"Yeh. They're living in your pa's old house. Phin and his bunch just plain took over the new one."

It wasn't exactly new, Jesse had thought, but he reckoned it was one way of distinguishing the original Ramsey home that his father had built from the larger one built later.

"I'll bet Elvira hates that," he'd said, thinking of Curt's wife.

Barnaby had looked at him sharply. A

tall, lean-faced, bearded man with a trailing handlebar mustache, he had thrust his hands into overall pockets and frowned.

"I reckon you're talking about Curt's woman. Hell, Jesse, she died some years ago. Didn't you know that?"

"No, hadn't heard," Jesse replied with no noticeable reaction.

He had seen Hannah to the inn, a small hostelry a short distance up the street where he felt she'd be safe and away from the usual hotel-saloon crowd. Barnaby had understood Jesse's explanation as to the ownership of the two horses they were riding, and promised to advise the town marshal of the situation since Ramsey was in a hurry to reach Crosshatch.

"You go mighty careful now," the stableman had warned. "That's a mean bunch of renegades you're dealing with. They don't know nothing but hell-raising and killing."

"Obliged to you for telling me," Jesse had said as he wheeled his horse about. The warning was unnecessary; he already had a pretty good idea of the situation at Crosshatch.

"You know if my brother Boone has rode in, too?"

Barnaby shook his head. "Ain't seen him, but I expect he could have if he got the word."

Jesse shrugged. "That could be the kink in the rope. It just could be that Jubilee wasn't able to get in touch with him. *Adiós.*"

"*Adiós*—and good luck," the stableman said, and Ramsey rode off.

Jesse, following an old trail with which he was familiar, swung north of the settlement, intending to come into Crosshatch from that direction. Most of the cattle and the hands looking after them would be to the south and west of the ranch at that time of the year, and he would as soon not encounter any of them until he had first talked things over with Curt and Jubilee.

He recalled what Barnaby had said about Elvira. Jesse endeavored to muster a strain of remorse for the woman's death, for Curt's sake, but it came hard. Still, he guessed he owed the spiteful woman a measure of thanks for driving him off. It had put him on his own, which eventually led to a good life as the owner of fine saloon and gambling house.

And it had also brought Ruby Bellman and him together. Someday he'd make Ruby his wife . . . Someday . . . Jesse sleeved away the sweat on his forehead. What about Ruby now that he'd met Hannah Bradley? Was Ruby still the woman he wanted to marry, or had matters changed and Hannah Bradley become the one he wanted at his side for the rest of his life? He was going to have to make a choice, one that would be most difficult—but one that would have to wait until the trouble at Crosshatch had been settled and the ranch was again the property of the Ramseys.

Back off to the east the crackle of gunshots sounded. Jesse slowed his mount and considered them. They were too far east for the ranch to mean trouble there, he saw, lining up a couple of familiar landmarks. Evidently it was someone shooting at a coyote or perhaps a cougar. More shots came a short time later, after he'd moved on, but he gave them no thought. Instead he was engrossed in the land, the grassy flats, the low hills, the gradual slopes that led up to Cooke's Peak, rising like a clenched fist out of the sun-baked soil.

The old California Stagecoach Trail running toward it was still visible—deep-cut ruts that were long ago abandoned but had resisted the efforts of the wind and persistent bunch grass to erase them.

Rabbits were plentiful, he saw, and the remembrance of how, when the ranch was young, they were the principal fare of the family. Dove, lark, and blue quail were plentiful, too, and once he saw a great Mexican eagle perched on the top limb of a paloverde. The raptor eyed his approach with fierce yellow eyes and lunged off into flight only after Jesse was within a few yards.

Reaching a wide arroyo familiar to him, Jesse began to veer south. He was well behind the ranch house and other structures by then, he knew. It would be prudent to angle toward the place at this point. A coyote, tail hanging low, jaws open, and tongue out as he panted for air, slunk off into a stand of nearby brush.

The wild dog had been in no great hurry, as was usual with them. Evidently there had been no cattle grazing on the range for some time, and consequently no cowhands. That part of the ranch, Jesse remembered, while not a part of the original deeded ranch, had, as the custom was, simply been acquired by his father as the need arose—free range, Jesse thought it was called.

Abruptly Jesse drew to a stop. He had topped out a rise, and a half mile ahead and below lay the ranch. He could see no activity on the hardpack that lay between the new house and the old, and the only sign of habitation was a trickle of gray smoke rising from the cookshack, old Calderone's domain. It brought a smile to Jesse Ramsey's face when he recalled how the bandy-legged old Mexican, who had never seemed young, would chase him and Boone off when they endeavored to get their hands on a tasty dried apple or peach pie cooling on a window shelf. Was Calderone still there—or had he fled when the outlaws took over?

Drumming his heels into the ribs of his horse, Jesse rode down the slope. The sooner he got off high ground, the less the chances were he'd been seen—and he'd like to keep it that way until he had a chance to talk to Curt. There was a buckboard drawn up behind the old house and a couple of horses standing in the lean-to shed nearby. A half dozen more were now visible, pulled up to the hitch rack of the new house, waiting slack-hipped for their riders to call upon them.

Keeping his mount to a walk, Jesse rode in behind the old house and stabled his horse in the shed with the others. Then, with a final glance across the hardpack, he crossed to the back door of the structure, tripped the thumb latch in the thick panel, and entered.

Curt was slouched, dozing in a large leather and wood chair, head on a pillow. Jubilee Jackson, busy preparing something for the evening meal at the counter behind the stove, came about suddenly at Jesse's unexpected entrance, his gnarled, bony hand reaching for the shotgun propped against the wall. Midway he paused, a smile slowly widening on his lips.

"Jesse! By God, it's you, ain't it!" he said in a loud happy voice. "I knowed you'd come!"

The older man stepped forward hurriedly and threw his arms about Ramsey, clapping him soundly on the back. "I told Curt you would!"

Jubilee pulled back and glanced at the older Ramsey. His boisterous greeting had awakened Curt, who was now staring at Jesse with expressionless eyes.

"Howdy, Curt," the younger man said, crossing the room and extending his hand.

Ramsey took his brother's fingers in a limp grasp. "You was a long time getting here," he said tonelessly. "Could be you're too damn late."

"Started the day I got Jubilee's message,"

Jesse said stiffly, freeing his hand. The old hostility was still there, he realized as he dropped back. Curt was many years older, and looked every bit of it, thanks to the accident which evidently had left him in a bad way. Regardless of Curt's attitude, he reckoned he should show a little compassion.

"Was right sorry to hear about Elvira," he said. "Barnaby at the stables told me—"

"Yeah, I'll just bet you're sorry!" Curt broke in acidly. "You never liked her, and she sure'n hell never had no use for you. Don't go making it out that it was any different."

Jesse's mouth pulled down into a humorless grin. "Can see you haven't changed any," he said, and turned his attention to Jubilee. "Heard anything from Boone?"

The old man wagged his head. "Nothing. Was shooting in the dark for him same as I was for you when I sent them letters and put out the word for you to come home. Boy, I'd about give you up."

"Letter was a long time tracking me down—I'm real surprised it ever found me," Jesse said, glancing about the room. "How long have you been cooped up in here? Can remember when we used this place for storing feed."

"Ain't been long," Curt said before Jubilee could reply. "Other house got too small for Durbin's bunch and us."

"Calderone says they've tore it up good inside," Jubilee said. "Ain't none of them doing any work, just lay around drinking and playing cards all the time—when they ain't fooling around with some of the town women."

"Have you tried talking to Durbin—making him some kind of a deal?"

"Hell, yes!" Curt shouted angrily. "You think I've just been setting here on my ass doing nothing? Hell, it ain't been but a couple of hours that I—"

"Somebody's coming," Jubilee interrupted and, taking up the shotgun, crossed to the doorway. He stood motionless for a long minute and then, grinning broadly, spun about.

"It's Boone—damn if it ain't!" he said. "And he's riding straight across the yard just like he owned the place."

"Boone?" Curt murmured. "You sure it's him?"

"You're dang right—and he's got a gal

with him. Redheaded—and she's sure a looker!"

22

"Just what you'd expect from him—bringing some hussy along," Curt muttered. "Was all he ever thought about—fooling around with a woman."

"Hell, he weren't no worse than any other young buck all full of vinegar and rearing to sow some wild oats," Jubilee said defensively.

Jesse smiled, remembering the days when he and Boone were growing into manhood. Moving to the doorway, he glanced out. Two men were standing on the porch of the new house and were watching Boone and the woman ride slowly, indifferently across the hardpack. The years hadn't changed Boone—that was certain. He was always one to flaunt his defiance.

"That dang fool," Jubilee muttered admiringly at the younger Ramsey's shoulder. "Reckon Durbin and his bunch knows now that they don't mean shucks to him!"

"He's a fool all right," Curt said flatly. "Could get himself a bullet in the back, showing off like that! That bunch don't hold off at doing anything they want. Any of them out there watching him?"

"A couple," Jesse said. "Standing out on the porch."

"Better keep an eye on them. They're just as apt to draw their guns and start shooting at him as they are to draw their next breath."

"I'm keeping an eye on them," Jesse said quietly.

Boone and his woman companion reached the old house, rounded the corner, and pulled up to the hitch rack at its rear. Jubilee hurriedly crossed the room and flung back the door for them.

"Boone!" the older man yelled. "You're sure a sight for sore eyes."

"Same here, old man," Boone said as, with the woman, he entered the room. He nodded briefly to Curt and to Jesse and then, placing an arm about the woman, added: "Like for you to meet Zoe Tillman."

Jubilee stepped forward, offered his hand. Curt only nodded while Jesse, still keeping a watchful eye on the outlaws on the porch, smiled and touched the brim of his hat with a forefinger.

"Took you long enough to get here, too,"

Curt said, brusquely. "Can see why—you been lollygagging all the way."

"I was a far piece up the line—Colorado—and I had a couple of things to do on the way down," Boone said.

A silence, heavy with tension, filled the room. Boone studied Curt for a long moment, and when he finally spoke his voice had the cutting edge of a Green River knife.

"Out of respect for Ma I won't call you a sonofabitch, but that's what you are—"

Curt thrashed about, endeavoring to sit up in his chair. His eyes were bright and his face worked with anger. "If I had my legs you'd not get away with saying that!"

"Doubt if it'd make any difference," Boone said. "You never did have the guts of a rabbit—always left the tough things up to your wife." He paused, looked around. "Where is Elvira? She get a bellyful of you and take off, too?"

"She's dead, son," Jubilee said quietly.

Boone's hard cornered face did not change. He could care less about Elvira. The scars she had inflicted upon him before he'd taken leave ran deep and nothing—not even her passing—would ever completely heal them.

"I reckon you can see what you and

Jesse's running off has brought us to," Curt said. "If you'd stayed here where you belong this never—"

"Don't go trying to blame it on Jesse and me," Boone snapped. "Anything that happened was brought on by your own doings."

"You think I made that horse fall on me, cripple me all up like I am?"

Boone shrugged, glanced at Zoe, standing quietly off to one side. She smiled faintly as he caught her eye. "How would I know? You never was much with a horse—never did treat one right."

Curt swore, struggled again to change his position in the chair. Boone glanced again at the woman.

"You can see how things are with me and my brothers," he said with a smile. "Just one big happy family." Moving by Curt, he crossed to the doorway. "Something special going on out there?"

"You stirred up the place a bit," Jesse said as they exchanged closer looks. "Sure glad you made it."

Boone shrugged. "I'm not down here to help Curt, I'm here for Pa and Ma's sake. Far as I'm concerned, Curt's the one that got himself into this fix, whatever it is, and we ought to damn well let him get himself out of it . . . You know what it's all about? Got a little of it from a bartender in Cruces, but not the whole story."

"I'm a little short on the knowing, too, but I expect Jubilee'll give us the straight of it," Jesse said, and turned to the old man. "We want to know what's going on here—"

Jubilee glanced toward the new house. "Looks like you riding in like you done, Boone, sure has got that bunch to worrying a mite," he said, and then launched into a full account of what had taken place to bring about present conditions at Crosshatch.

"Expect it ought to be said that it all sort of began when Curt got himself hurt, and then got worse when George Coe was shot in the back. Been hell ever since," he finished in a low voice.

"And you say this Durbin and his bunch sold off the whole herd?"

"Was told to sell off a thousand. Right now I'm betting we ain't got a dozen head left on the place."

Jesse rubbed at his jaw. "How the hell could Durbin pull off a deal like that?"

"Curt had give him papers for the thousand head of stock he aimed to sell. Durbin changed them when he got to the railhead."

Boone swore. "What the hell! Wasn't

there any of the cowhands on the drive loyal to Crosshatch?"

"Durbin had done got rid of all the ones who wouldn't throw in with him."

"That figures," Boone muttered.

"What're you all talking about?" Curt broke in impatiently. "Something you ain't wanting me to know? I don't like for anybody to be going behind my back."

"We're not," Jesse said. "Jubilee's just telling us the straight of things. You know where the money is that Durbin got for your herd?"

Curt shrugged as Boone and Jesse moved back to face him. He motioned to Zoe.

"Get some coffee on the stove, woman. You might as well be of some use instead of just standing there."

Boone glanced at Zoe, shook his head, an indication she was under no obligation to take orders from the eldest Ramsey, but she only smiled and turned to the stove. Boone turned back to Curt.

"Asked you about the money. Three thousand head would bring a pile of cash."

"Around fifty thousand dollars—maybe a little more," Curt said. "Steers were bringing eighteen to twenty dollars a head. He's got the money with him."

"A draft?" Jesse asked, glancing out the door toward the new house. "Jube, you mind keeping an eye on that bunch while Boone and I get this straight?"

Jackson crossed quickly to the doorway and took up a stand.

"He had a draft," Curt said, "but he's cashed it."

"Looks like he's aiming to pull out," Boone said with a glance at Jesse. "Expect we got here just in time."

"There's Phin coming in now," Jubilee said, pointing.

Jesse and Boone crossed to the older man's side. Two riders had pulled up the hitch rack of the new house, and were dismounting. One, a stockily built man, cigar stuck into a corner of his mouth, looked about the yard and said something to his companion. Both laughed.

"That's Durbin, the one with the stogie," Jubilee said. "Wearing new duds! Looks like he went to town and bought hisself a whole new outfit—boots and all. And Bill Toon, he's the gent with him—he's got hisself a new hat."

The lid on the coffeepot began to rattle as water inside it started to boil. Zoe, searching about for cups, had located three and was setting out several small bowls as substitutes for the shortage. The can of sugar was alongside them, as were spoons.

"Where do you keep the milk?" she asked.

"Don't use it," Curt snapped. "Take it black. We all do."

Zoe, having added a measure of ground beans to the water in the pot, smiled sweetly at him. "Coffee will be ready in only a minute or so," she said.

Curt muttered something and looked up at Boone. "Well, you got any ideas? What are you aiming to do about Durbin—and my money? If you let him get away with what he's done, I'll be dead broke—and Crosshatch won't be worth nothing."

There was a silence for several moments, broken finally by Jesse. "Why didn't you go to the law when this first started—when Coe got shot?"

"Talked to the deputy—didn't have no marshal, still don't. He'd just quit and the town hadn't been able to hire on another'n. Deputy who took over couldn't do anything about it. Was too scared of Durbin and his crowd, I figure."

"How about the other ranchers? Folks

always used to pitch in and help when asked."

"They've got their own troubles—and things've changed around here since you left, Jesse. Nowadays it's up to a man to skin his own snakes."

Zoe paused, turned around. "You mean neighbors in this part of the country never help each other—they just look the other way when somebody's in trouble?"

"Little hard to do much helping when folks live ten or maybe twenty miles apart," Curt said dryly. "Henry Trigg's the closest—about ten miles to the north. Talked to him, but he wouldn't promise to side me if I made a move against Durbin. Had his own problems with rustlers—and he couldn't keep a crew."

"How many in Durbin's bunch?" Boone asked.

"Maybe a dozen," Jubilee replied.

"They all there in the house?"

"Can't be sure," the older man said. "Expect about half of them are in town. They do a lot of hanging around the saloons."

"Come across three of them on the way here," Boone said. "Was in the brakes. You don't need to count them."

"You have a shoot-out with them?" Jesse

210

wondered. "I heard shooting over in that direction."

Boone nodded. "Put two of them under. Let the third one go. Was just a kid."

"Probably the Casey boy," Jubilee said. "Any chance he might come back?"

"Got my doubts," Boone said. "From what you say, it looks like we'll be going up against at least half of Durbin's bunch—maybe a couple more."

"The way I count it up, too," Jesse said. "What've you got in mind?"

Boone walked to the doorway and glanced toward the new house. "Only thing we can—have it out with them."

"A shoot-out?" Curt said, frowning.

"You got a better idea?"

The eldest Ramsey shook his head. "No, reckon not, but the odds are sure bad."

"Maybe not. We'll wait a couple more hours. Sun will be in their eyes when they come out of the house, and behind us. That'll give us the edge—and that's all we'll need."

"Coffee's ready," Zoe announced.

Jesse deliberately turned his back to her and faced Boone. "Your lady friend know what we're aiming to do—two of us going

211

up against six or eight killers?" he asked in a low voice.

"There'll be three of us," Jubilee said quietly.

"Four," Curt added. "Don't count me out of it."

Boone made no comment. Jesse nodded and Jubilee Jackson grinned broadly. "That's the way it ought to be—a family standing by each other."

Jesse continued to stare at Boone. "You answering my question?"

Ramsey's shoulders stirred. "I reckon she does—she can see how things stack up around here. Like as not, I'll have to lock her up in the shed to keep her out of the shoot-out."

"Sounds like a lot of woman. You aim to marry her?"

"What I'm thinking—"

A half smile parted Jesse's lips. "Sure a hell of a way to welcome a bride into a family!"

23

Boone raised his eyes to the sun. He and Zoe had stepped out of the house and were in the small clearing behind it. Curt's constant carping and upbraiding had eventually worn thin, and they had left the old house and moved off into the shade of the lean-to shed where the horses were tethered to get away from him.

"Expect the time's about right," he said.

Zoe followed his upward glance. At the angle the sun now was, its strong, bright rays would be slanting into the face of the outlaws when they came out of the new house. She laid a hand on his muscular forearm.

"I know it's foolish to say this, but are you sure of what you're planning to do?"

"Can't ever be dead sure of anything in this life but we'll have the advantage, and that's what I always look for at a time like this. Besides, I can't think of any other way to deal with them other'n to burn the house down—and if I did that Curt would really have something to yell about."

"Maybe you and Jesse are going too far out on a limb for him—"

"Could be. The point to me is that I'm not doing it so much for him as I am for Ma and Pa—he's just sort of looking after it, or supposed to be. I can't forget they starved and bled to build this ranch, and I'm damned if I'll stand by and let a bunch of outlaws have it. Jesse ain't said so, but I expect he feels the same, else he wouldn't be here."

"Boone!" Curt's peevish voice cut through the warm, afternoon hush. "Ain't you about done out there? I thought you was here to do something about Durbin and his bunch."

Boone made no reply, only grinned wryly. Reaching out, he took Zoe in his arms and held her close.

"Want you to stay inside the house," he said sternly. "Want you to do what I tell you this time—I've got big plans for us when this is all over."

Zoe smiled, put her arms about him and, drawing him close, kissed him. "I've got plans, too, so don't take any chances out there."

"You can bet on it—"

"I don't know exactly what you mean to

do, and I guess it's best that I don't—but come back, Boone. I've learned that I need you—and I don't think I want to live without you."

"I'll be back," he said, pulling back. "The bullet hasn't been molded yet that's got my name on it . . . Now mind what I've told you—stay inside out of harm's way."

Together they walked to the rear of the old house and entered. All three men turned to face them.

"Ain't no time to be spooning," Curt said sourly. "You're counting on the sun. Could be you've waited too long."

"No, I figure it's in just about the right place," Boone answered coolly. "All of you know what we'll be up against, I reckon."

Jubilee nodded. Jesse's shoulders twitched. "Only way I can see to do it."

"Same here," Boone said. "It'll be best for me to walk a bit ahead and do the talking. There're two buildings standing in the yard between us and them—the outhouse and the wagon shed. They're about ten foot apart."

"You figuring on using them?" Jesse asked. "I thought—"

"You figured we'd buck them head on, that it? Well, that's about what we'll be doing, only I don't aim to make it easy for them."

"Come on, come on, get down to hard rock," Curt muttered. "You seem to be running this—what do you want us to do?"

"Us? What the hell good can you do?" Boone asked with an impatient shake of his head. "Best thing you can do is keep back."

"Like hell I will!" the eldest Ramsey shouted. "I can shoot a rifle good as the next man—just have to do it setting down in a wheelbarrow. You're forgetting I've got a bigger stake in this than anybody."

Boone started to reply, but Jubilee spoke up first, cutting him off. "I'll look after Curt. You just say what you want us to do—all of us, including him."

"Up to you," Boone said indifferently. "What I figure we best do is all go out together and make a stand between the wagon shed and the outhouse. I'll holler for Durbin to come out. I'm planning on the rest of his bunch coming out with him, either because he'll tell them to, or they'll be curious and want to see what's going on."

"Expect there's the big catch. Some of them are likely to stay inside," Jubilee said.

"The whole thing's mighty risky the way

I see it," Curt remarked. "We're going to be setting ducks out there in the open."

"Not if we handle it right. There's a reason I picked the spot between the shed and the outhouse to make a stand. When I get Durbin and his bunch outside and the shooting starts, I want you, Jesse, to jump in behind the shed. Jubilee, you and Curt take shelter behind the outhouse."

A muffled gasp came from Zoe Tillman. The men remained silent for several moments, and then Jubilee broke the quiet.

"Now, just what'll you be doing?"

Boone grinned. "Shooting back," he said. "Don't get all puckered up about me. I've been down this road before. Have you all got it straight?"

"What's your woman going to be doing?" Curt asked, nodding at the redhead as Jubilee brought over the wheelbarrow for his use.

"She'll be staying right here inside the house," Boone said flatly. "I won't have her out where she can get hurt."

"Why not?" Curt demanded as Jubilee lifted him from his chair and placed him in the makeshift conveyance. "She's going to be a part of the family—and we could sure use another rifle."

"She'll be a part of the family all right, and I aim to keep her alive for that," Boone snapped. "Anybody else got something to say?"

There was no response. Jesse moved to the doorway and glanced out. Jubilee handed Curt his rifle and, cramming a handful of spare shotgun shells into his own jacket pocket, took up his scattergun and passed it to Curt also.

"You'll have to hold old Betsy for me till we get out yonder."

Curt accepted the double-barrel and gestured at Boone. "Come on, let's get this over with one way or another."

Boone smiled at Zoe and moved to where Jesse stood. He looked back at Jubilee, who had taken up the handles of the wheelbarrow and was having some difficulty in turning it about.

"You needing help with that thing?"

"Nope," the older man said. "And don't go fretting over me. You just look out for yourself."

Boone stepped out onto the bleached, wooden landing that fronted the old house and then down onto the hardpack. Jesse, one hand riding the butt of the .45 hanging at his hip, followed closely. They halted briefly, waiting for Jubilee to wheel Curt through the doorway, and then, abreast, made their way to the space between the two small structures Boone had designated. When they were lined up, still abreast, Boone stepped forward a few paces. Drawing his gun, he glanced at the others.

"*Buena suerte,*" he said softly.

"Same to you," Jesse and Jubilee replied in chorus.

Turning his attention briefly toward the old house as if to see that Zoe was safe inside, he raised his weapon and fired a shot into the air. As the echoes rolled out across the late afternoon hush, and without conscious thought he replaced the spent cartridge, he fixed his eyes on the back door of the new house.

"Durbin! Come out—it's settling-up time!"

Almost immediately two men appeared on the porch. Ramsey, a tall shape at the edge of the shadows cast by the wagon shed, turned his head slightly toward Jubilee but did not take his eyes off the outlaws.

"Ain't neither one of them Durbin," Jubilee said. "He'll be the one wearing new duds."

"I remember," Boone said. "You know who these two are?"

"Nope—just a couple of his gunnies."

"Durbin—come on out or we'll burn the place down!"

Curt muttered something at low breath. Boone smiled. The last thing he wanted to do was set fire to the home that his folks, assisted by him and his brothers, had put so much sweat and hard labor into building, but he needed something to bring out the outlaw.

"There he is," Jubilee said abruptly. "He's that real fancy-looking jasper."

"Bought all them clothes with my money," Curt muttered. "I'd like to blow the goddamn bastard's head off!"

"Just sit quiet and maybe you'll get your chance," Jesse said.

Durbin, taking a place between his two friends, pushed his hat forward as a shield against the sun. "Who're you and what the hell do you want?"

"I'm another Ramsey—Curt's brother. Man to my left is Jesse, another brother. Expect you know our uncle, Jubilee."

"Sure I know him," Durbin said, stepping down off the porch.

Other members of Durbin's crew were

putting in their appearance, two of them following the outlaw down into the yard while three more took up widely separate positions on the porch.

"Seven," Jubilee said. "That sure ain't all of them, counting Phin. Must be at least three of them in town."

"We'll have to figure it that way—"

"What do you want?" Durbin called across the strip of hardpack lying between them.

"You know the answer to that—we want the money you got from selling the herd. After that we want you and your bunch to pack up and get off Ramsey land."

Durbin pulled off his hat and ran stubby fingers through his brick-red hair. "You don't say! You sure ain't wanting much."

"Only what's rightfully our—"

"You say ours? The way I heard it, the cripple there owns the place."

"Crosshatch is a family ranch. Our pa built it—Curt runs it, and we aim to keep it in the family." Boone paused, glanced around. Tension hung over the yard like a thick cloud. "Are you handing over the money—better than fifty thousand dollars I'm told, or do we come in after it?"

"Come in after it—and be damned!"

Phin Durbin shouted and made a stab for his gun.

24

Boone drew and fired instantly. Durbin was moving away, however, and both his bullet and that of the outlaw missed. Elsewhere along the front of the new house other guns opened up as the remaining outlaws went into action.

Off to his right Boone heard the roar of Jubilee's shotgun and the crack of Curt's rifle. With smoke already hanging over the hardpack, Boone threw himself to the ground. Rolling to one side, he fired again at Phin Durbin. Two of the outlaws were down—the one at the north end of the porch, the other in the yard where he had been siding Durbin.

Jesse was triggering his weapon steadily from the side of the old wagon shed. Boone, now up against the structure, heard his six-gun click on a spent cartridge. At once he shoved the weapon into its holster and, jerking from his belt the weapon he'd taken from one of the outlaws who had tried to ambush him earlier, he resumed shooting.

Smoke was thickening and beginning to drift across the yard, mixing as it did with the pall of dust stirred up by Durbin's men as they dodged about endeavoring to avoid the hail of lead coming from the Ramseys and Jubilee Jackson. Boone heard Jesse curse, reckoned his younger brother had been hit. Too, Jubilee's scattergun had fallen silent, an indication the older man had also taken a bullet.

Grim, Boone narrowed his eyes trying to single out Phin Durbin. He saw him a moment or so later. The outlaw, one arm hanging loosely at his side, had backed his way up onto the porch of the house. He had been hit, that was evident, but he moved as if he were far from being out of the fight. Like as not, he had only a slight wound in the fleshy part of his arm and was not seriously injured.

Another of the outlaws on the porch staggered back, collided with the wall, and fell forward. Curt's rifle had accounted for him, as the sharp crack of the weapon during a lull in which only the frantic barking of the dogs was to be heard, had been the only gunshot.

Boone's spare gun was suddenly empty. He tossed it aside and, leaning back against the side of the wagonshed, began to thumb fresh cartridges from the loops in his gunbelt and reload.

"Jesse—you hit?" he called above the now-irregular cracking of guns.

"Some," his younger brother replied.

"Bad?"

"Nope. Just got me in the leg."

"Better work your way back up to the old house and let Zoe take care of it. I'll cover—"

"No, I'm not hurt all that bad. It can wait until we've got this settled . . . How about Curt and the old man?"

"Don't know about Curt, but Jubilee's not doing any shooting. Expect he's been hit, too."

The cylinder of his .45 again full, Boone turned his attention once more to the new house. Durbin was no longer to be seen, evidently having sought safety inside the structure. Another outlaw lay sprawled on the porch, and one of the two left in the yard was out of the shooting. Sitting flat in the dust, head hanging forward, gun on the ground beside him, he was rocking back and forth uncontrollably.

Abruptly two quick rifle shots broke out from somewhere near the old house. Boone swore. It had to be Zoe getting in on the shoot-out. A moment later he saw the reason: two of the outlaw bunch had left the shelter of the new house from its side, and had attempted to race across the short stretch of open ground lying to the north and reach a band of trees and brush growing there. Had they gained the safety of the thick growth, they would have been in a position to circle around, get in behind the wagon shed and the outhouse, and thus have him—along with Jesse, Curt, and Jubilee—trapped in a crossfire.

Boone grinned. The pair had failed to make it. One, dragging a wounded leg, had turned about and was struggling to reach the safety of the new house. His partner, apparently unharmed and having had enough of the shoot-out which was going the wrong way for the Durbin party, was running in long, loping strides for the hitch rack, where his horse evidently awaited him.

There'd be no more attempts on the part of the outlaws to circle around and gain an advantage in that manner, Boone thought —thanks to Zoe. He grinned tightly. What a woman! He'd never before gotten interested enough in one of her sex to consider marriage, but the redhead was different. One thing for damn sure—he'd never let her get away from him.

Through the heavy mix of dust and smoke Boone could see the ranch cook, Calderone, peering through the one window that faced the hardpack. The dogs were still barking, although there was no one still standing in the yard or the porch.

"Jubilee, Curt—you two all right?" he called.

"I ain't been shot if that's what you mean," Curt answered. "But Jube's been hit. Up in the shoulder, maybe pretty bad."

"Tell him to hang on a little longer. Jesse took a bullet, too."

"You hit?"

"No. I'm going into the house after Durbin. Pretty sure that's what happened to him."

"Yeh, I seen him go in. Watch your step. I expect you'll find a couple more of his bunch holed up in there with him."

Boone shook his head in wonderment. Having Curt express a note of concern for him was the last thing he would have expected.

"I'll keep my eyes peeled," he said,

checking his gun. "Give me some cover while I make a run for the house."

"Sure thing . . . You hear Boone, Jesse? Start shooting when you see him running."

Boone, hunched low, moved to the corner of the shed. He rode out a few moments, listening to the anxious nickering of a horse over behind the feed barn, and then, rising, gathered his muscles.

"Open up!" he yelled and broke into a run across the hardpack.

Jesse and Curt immediately began to lay down a steady barrage of bullets that thudded into the thick planks making up the back wall of the new house. Sprinting, Boone reached the porch, leaped across it, and drew up by the door. With a wave of his hand he silenced the guns of Jesse and Curt, realizing as he did that not one challenging shot had come from the outlaws. Were they all out of it—or were they just lying low, waiting for him? There was only one way to find out, he decided, and again, bent low, Boone darted through the open doorway into the house.

Recollection of the place flooded into his mind. The first room had been the family kitchen. Once it had contained a six-hole Belmont cookstove the nickle parts of which his mother had taken great pride in keeping shined. There had also been a large, round dining table around which several chairs —ten at least—were placed.

The walls had several shelves affixed to them from which his mother, and later Elvira, had hung curtains to conceal or protect the supply of foodstuffs, just which he never really knew.

Now there were only the table and the chairs, all showing the scars from countless poker games and whiskey bouts staged by the outlaws. The big cast-iron Belmont was missing, either having been moved to the cookshack or discarded.

Anger heightened by what he saw had taken place, Boone, keeping low and listening for sounds, edged toward the hallway that led deeper into the house—a parlor, three bedrooms, and a small corner cubicle that served as an office where his father, and later Curt, kept records of the herds and copies of business transactions. If he were to encounter trouble, it would come now, he reckoned, as he began to make his way along the corridor.

The scrape of a bootheel on the bare floor of the room directly ahead brought Ramsey to a stop. A moment later one of the outlaws lurched into view—gun in hand and ready to fire. Boone shot him without conscious thought, and as the smoke boiled up to fill the narrow hallway and the outlaw sank to the floor, he continued on with the echoes of the gunshot pounding at his ears. He wasn't interested in Durbin's men, only in the outlaw himself.

A sudden rattle of gunshots outside the house halted him again. Evidently one or more of the renegades had shown himself, perhaps trying to reach the hitch rack where the horses waited, and had drawn Jesse's fire. Boone knew it would have been his younger brother as the shots came from a handgun, not a rifle.

Boone moved on cautiously. Chances were good he'd just encountered the last outlaw in the house, other than Phin Durbin, but he could not afford to take such for granted. *Expect the worst and you won't be disappointed*, he recalled someone once said. Ready, gun lifted and cocked, he pressed on. He came to the last of the bedrooms. Empty, filled only with the pungent smell of powder smoke. Where the hell was Durbin? Had the outlaw succeeded in slipping out one of the windows or possibly the front door?

A faint noise at the end of the hallway brought Ramsey to alert. The office. There was someone in it. Crossing the smoke-hazed corridor, he drew up to the door. The sound came again, this time much louder and definitely created by a chair being pushed aside. Ramsey drew himself upright. Raising a leg, he drove a booted foot against the thin panel and sent it splintering inward on its hinges.

The crouched shape of Phin Durbin whirled. Gun up, the outlaw fired instantly. Boone, long schooled by experience in facing such moments and never caught unprepared or unready, triggered his own weapon in the same moment, or slightly before Durbin had gotten off his shot. Ramsey felt the outlaw's bullet sear across his ribs, setting up a groove of stinging pain and raising the smell of scorched cloth as it ripped through his shirt.

Durbin came completely about. The gun in his hand sagged as a shocked look crossed his broad, ruddy face. He seemed about to say something but no words came from his flaring lips, and then abruptly he began to sink to the floor, the tin box he was holding spilling its contents of currency, double eagles, and other coins at Boone Ramsey's feet.

25

"I expect that'll fix you up," the physician said, stepping back after administering to Jubilee. "Bullet hit the collarbone, broke it."

"How long's it going to take for it to heal?" Curt, slouched in his chair, asked.

"Can't say. Jubilee's tough as whang leather, but old bones mend slow. Main thing is for him to take it easy. I'll drop back by in a couple of days and see how he's doing."

"If he can't work and look after me, how'll I make out?" Curt grumbled. "Can't do nothing for myself."

"I took care of that when Zoe and me went into town," Boone said. "Put out the word that you'd be doing some hiring on. Some of your old hands that Durbin drove off were still hanging around. They'll be showing up in the morning."

"Won't be needing but a couple of men, leastwise I won't the way things are now," Curt said.

Earlier, after all of the shooting was over and the wounded Jesse and Jubilee had been brought back to the old house where Zoe could give them medical attention, Boone, with the redhaired woman, had ridden into Mesilla. There he had summoned the town physician and dispatched him immediately to the ranch. After that he'd hunted up the young marshal, instructed him to recruit some help, obtain a team and wagon, and go out to Crosshatch for the outlaws, some of whom were dead, some only wounded. Zoe, meanwhile, had gone on to the hotel in Las Cruces, where she planned to bid her aunts and uncles farewell.

"Ain't sure this place is worth building up again," Curt said when the doctor had gone. "And I've got all that money—"

"Up to you," Boone said indifferently, gazing out the window.

A sort of haze covered the flats and low hills, turning everything a pale gold and creating indefinite, mysterious shadows. Within another hour the sun would be gone, hidden behind the Burro Mountains to the west.

"That's the way I see it, too," Jesse said. "It's for you to decide . . . You ready to leave, Boone?"

"Reckon I am," Boone replied. "Zoe and me are getting married soon's we can rustle up a preacher. Then we're buying her a horse and some riding clothes—and heading north. What about you?"

"Think I'll rent myself a horse and buggy and drive down to El Paso for a spell—long enough for the soreness to leave my leg —then I'll be moving out for Texas. Got a saloon and a gambling business to look after."

"You've got a crease alongside your head, too, that don't look old. Been waiting for you to say how you got it, but you seem kind of bashful."

Jesse smiled, touched the livid streak above his left ear carefully. "Was a stage holdup. One of the outlaws took a shot at me. Come close to putting me under."

"What about him?" Jubilee, sprawled on a bunk at the south end of the room, wanted to know.

"He's dead—"

"Figures," Curt said dryly. "The both of you was always too handy with a gun . . . Thought maybe you'd both stay around for a spell."

"You can see we got other things to do,"

Jesse said. "We both came here to help you and Jubilee—and that's what we've done."

"And now we're leaving," Boone added, moving toward the door.

"Just one minute!" Jubilee said, drawing himself up on one elbow. "Don't look like Curt's going to say it, but I sure will. Me and him are mighty grateful to you. Your pa and ma would be real proud of the way you Ramseys—all three of you—stood there side by side and shot it out with them outlaws."

"You had a hand in it, too," Boone said.

"We all did," the old man said, settling back. "We was a family there again for a spell—just the way it ought to be."

Curt nodded. "Yeah—the way it ought to be. I ain't much for words, but I want you to know that I'm thankful to you both. One third of that cash belongs to each of you. I'm ready to pay off."

"Forget it," Boone said. "It's rightfully yours—you done all the work after I rode off."

"You can keep my third, too," Jesse said. "I don't need it and I don't want it."

"I see. Well, if you ever want to settle down and come back, the place'll be here," the older man said and extended his hand to Jesse. "Have a care."

"Sure will," the youngest Ramsey said, taking Curt's fingers into his own. "Goes for you, too, Uncle," he said and, limping badly, crossed to where Jubilee lay and shook his hand.

"So long, old man," Boone said, also pausing beside Jackson's bunk. Patting him gently on the uninjured shoulder, he added: "You for damn sure better do what the doc told you!"

Jubilee smiled, but there was no humor in his expression, only a sadness. "Aim to."

The middle Ramsey turned, nodded to the eldest, and started toward the door where Jesse was now waiting.

"Boone—"

At Curt's voice he hesitated and looked around. "Yeah?"

"Will you take my hand?"

For a long breath the bounty hunter stood motionless and then, turning, took his older brother's hand in a firm grasp, and grinned.

"*Adios, hermano*," he said softly in Spanish, and followed Jesse out into the yard.